TOPSPIN

orca sports

TOPSPIN

SONYA SPREEN BATES

ORCA BOOK PUBLISHERS

Library and Archives Canada Cataloguing in Publication

Bates, Sonya Spreen, author
Topspin / Sonya Spreen Bates.
(Orca sports)

Issued in print and electronic formats.
ISBN 978-1-4598-0385-5 (pbk.).-- ISBN 978-1-4598-0647-4 (bound)
ISBN 978-1-4598-0386-2 (pdf). -- ISBN 978-1-4598-0387-9 (epub)

I. Title. II. Series: Orca sports
PS8603.A8486T66 2013   jc813'.6   C2013-902338-0
                                                C2013-902339-9

First published in the United States, 2013
Library of Congress Control Number: 2013937056

Summary: At a junior tournament in Melbourne, Kat finds herself caught in the
middle of a plot to sabotage the star tennis player.

*Orca Book Publishers is dedicated to preserving the environment and has printed
this book on Forest Stewardship Council® certified paper.*

Orca Book Publishers gratefully acknowledges the support for its publishing
programs provided by the following agencies: the Government of Canada through
the Canada Book Fund and the Canada Council for the Arts, and the Province of
British Columbia through the BC Arts Council and
the Book Publishing Tax Credit.

Cover photography by Getty Images

ORCA BOOK PUBLISHERS
PO Box 5626, Stn. B
Victoria, BC Canada
V8R 6S4

ORCA BOOK PUBLISHERS
PO Box 468
Custer, WA USA
98240-0468

www.orcabook.com
Printed and bound in Canada.

16 15 14 13 • 4 3 2 1

For my daughters, Meg and Claudia

chapter one

Melbourne Park. Home of the Australian Open tennis tournament. Three main arenas, retractable roofs, commentator boxes, seven indoor courts, eighteen outdoor courts, warm-up areas, change rooms, pro shop, souvenir shops. All the greats have played here. Roger Federer, Rafael Nadal, Serena Williams, Victoria Azarenka...and me?

Okay. So this wasn't the Australian Open. It was a bronze-level tournament in the Optus Junior Tour. And I wasn't Victoria Azarenka or ever likely to be. But the only time I'd seen anything remotely like this tennis complex was when I went to the US Open in New York. As a spectator, not a competitor. Now here I was. At Melbourne Park. As a competitor.

I am a self-confessed tennis junkie. I started playing back in Vancouver when I was six. My parents wanted me to play softball, but after I struck out every time at bat for a whole season, they decided maybe I needed a different sport. As soon as they put a tennis racket in my hand, I was hooked. I haven't looked back since.

Not even when we moved to Sydney, Australia, six months ago. I'd been studying for final exams, training twice a week with Evelyn Ferguson and looking forward to a camping trip with Margie up at Whistler when school let out. Then Dad got a job offer, and everything spun out of control. Instead of mountain biking down Whistler Mountain, I'd landed at Rothmore High, repeating half of grade eleven and getting laughed at every five minutes for things I'd never even known existed. I mean, how was I supposed to know that "The Man from Snowy River" was a poem before it was a movie? Or that ANZAC was an acronym for the Australian and New Zealand armies who fought in WWI? Who knew there was such a thing as Australian rules football? Or that there were two different kinds of rugby?

What I did know, though, was tennis. In Australia, tennis was a year-round sport. And Hugo Mansfield had agreed to coach me and set me up as Miri Tregenza's doubles partner. So here I was in Melbourne, preparing to compete on the very courts I'd seen so many times on TV. To be honest, it was rather intimidating. Not that we were going to play in the main arenas or anything, but still.

It was the day before the start of the tournament. We'd flown in that morning, and our courts were booked for our final training session. There were four of us—me, Miri, Hugo and his star player, Hamish Brown.

It still felt kind of unreal that I was there at all. Hugo was the best junior coach in Sydney. Even I knew that, and I'd only lived there a few months. He trained a couple of kids at our club, but he didn't take just anyone. You had to be serious about your tennis, and you had to be good. Scary good. I was under no illusions that I was in that category. I wasn't Wimbledon material, but I loved the game. It was only good luck on my part that Miri's doubles partner had injured her shoulder and was out for the rest of the season. Leaving Miri looking for a new partner. Enter stage right, me, Kat McDonald. That was a month ago, and now I had the next few days to prove to Hugo that he hadn't wasted his time on me.

It was a cold, overcast September afternoon, the beginning of spring, but it felt more like winter. No rain, which was lucky. I guess the rain in Sydney hadn't reached Melbourne yet. I still wasn't used to the reversed seasons. September and spring didn't compute in my mind, but there it was.

And despite North Americans' illusion that Australia is hot all the time, winter in Sydney had been cold. Not cold-cold like Toronto or Calgary, but cold and wet. A bit like Vancouver. It felt good to be out and moving.

I'd had a peek at the other kids as we'd walked through the courts. They all looked awesome, running drills or hitting serve after serve perfectly over the net. Miri and Hamish didn't seem fazed by it. They'd both been playing the junior circuit for three years. I guess they'd played here at Melbourne Park plenty of times, and besides, they had a couple of days before the main tournament started. For me, qualifying rounds started the next day. I was a bundle of nerves.

Hamish popped the ball over to Hugo and we started a rally. This was the first time I'd been on the court with Hamish. He had an awesome backhand. It never seemed to miss. And he was almost unbeatable at the net. His reach was so long, he got to the tramlines with a single step.

He'd made it to the quarterfinals in the Australian Open Juniors last year, and I could see why.

I, on the other hand, was a total disaster. I messed up the first two shots. Easy forehands that flew long when I wasn't even trying to send the ball deep.

Miri threw her hands up in disgust. I think I was fulfilling her worst nightmare. She had never wanted me for a partner in the first place. The first time we trained together, she eyed me like a piece of rotten fish. But beggars can't be choosers, and she was stuck with me for the duration of the tournament.

Not that she didn't have reason to be frustrated. Miri Tregenza was like a shadow image of Maria Sharapova, tall and slim but with jet-black hair and olive skin that never turned bright red after a match like mine did. She played like Sharapova, too, minus the screeching. Hard-hitting and aggressive, she never let an opportunity slip by. She was one of the top seeds for the tournament—I think she was ranked number two to win. I knew she thought I was going to bring her down.

"Come on, Kat, concentrate," Hugo said.

I tried to block everything out. Concentrate on the ball. Miri lobbed one onto my forehand and I shuffled into position. Backswing, follow through. The ball slammed onto my racket and arced perfectly over the net. Okay, now we were in business.

We rallied back and forth. A couple of shots went wild, but I tried not to let it get to me. I just concentrated on the next one. Topspin forehand. Shuffle back to center. Backhand slice. Move into the net and volley. Lob. Overhead smash. After awhile my brain switched off and my body took over, moving instinctively, anticipating the next shot. I felt good. Light, quick, powerful.

Before I knew it, Hugo called time.

"All right," he said. "You're ready. Get your stuff and we'll head to the hotel."

chapter two

With the rest of the day off, I headed back to Melbourne Park after checking into the hotel. It was only a short walk, and I wanted to get my bearings so I knew where I was going the next day. I also wanted to get a better look at my competition. Maybe that was a bad idea. Maybe I was freaking myself out for no reason, but it seemed important to know what I was up against.

According to the schedule, I was on court 12 at eight thirty, playing a girl named

Amelia Barrett. Not that that helped me any. I wouldn't know Amelia Barrett if I ran her over with a ten-ton truck. But I could find court 12, and I could check out all the girls who were still training. If I beat this Amelia, I'd be up against the others anyway.

I bought some sushi and a bottle of water at one of the vendors and meandered through the courts. There were some really good tennis players out there. I mean, they were all juniors, like me, but some really stood out. They were the stars of the future, no doubt about it. There were also some who were more at my level. They didn't have quite the speed, power or accuracy. There was a weak backhand here and there, a flubbed volley. I could only hope they weren't all in the divisions for younger players.

When I got to court 12, I stopped to watch. There were two girls on the court who looked about my age. A tall blond girl with legs up to her armpits, and a shortish kid who looked a little younger, with short spiky hair. The blond girl tossed the ball up for a serve, brought her racket around and slammed it over the net for an ace. I hoped she wasn't Amelia Barrett.

I continued my wandering, heading behind the courts to where the shops were set up—a souvenir shop selling T-shirts and caps, a place to have rackets restrung, even a booth where you could clock the speed of your serve. The results were displayed on an electronic board above the backstop: 143 kilometers per hour, 152, 115, 127. I didn't think I'd give it a try. No need to demoralize myself this close to the tournament.

As I left the booth, I spotted Miri and Hamish near the food stalls. I started toward them, then changed my mind. They were deep in conversation, and Miri didn't look happy. Quite honestly, I didn't know why they were going out. Miri had been in a bad mood since the flight to Melbourne that morning. And it didn't seem like Hamish was enjoying her company any more than I was. But it was none of my business. I turned the other way and went back to the courts.

It became my business when Miri missed curfew that night. She wasn't in the room when I got back. I didn't think anything of it. It was still early, and I wasn't Miri's babysitter. But as it got closer and closer to 10:00 PM, when Hugo would be coming around to check on us, I started to get worried. Where was she, and what was she doing? Had something happened to her?

At one minute to ten I got a text message. **On my way. Cover for me. Miri.**

Great. Now what should I do?

There was a knock on the door. I went to answer it, my mind racing. Did I cover for Miri and risk getting into Hugo's bad books if he found out? Or did I tell him she wasn't here and suffer Miri's wrath for the rest of the tournament? Not an easy choice.

"Everything set for tomorrow?" Hugo said, brushing past me into the room without being invited. "Where's Miri?"

"She's...uh...in the bathroom," I said.

He glanced around. Luckily, the bathroom door was closed, so he couldn't see she wasn't there.

"Oh. Well, about tomorrow," he said. "We'll go to the courts early so you can have a bit of a hit before it all gets going. Get the bugs out. And don't worry about Amelia Barrett. She's a little shrimp of a thing. No backhand. You'll beat her easy. Not that I want you to get overconfident. Remember what we talked about. Don't get rattled by the competition. You've got the goods. Just use it." He glanced at the bathroom door. "What's taking her so long?"

"You know...girl stuff," I said with a shrug.

He moved closer to the door, and I held my breath.

"Miri? On the courts at six thirty. Don't be late."

"We'll be there," I said quickly. To my profound relief, he headed out of our room, and I closed the door gratefully behind him.

Now, where was Miri?

chapter three

I was asleep, or close to it, when Miri finally
showed up. I heard her keycard in the lock,
and then she went into the bathroom.
The door thunked closed behind her.
I peered at the clock. Twelve forty.

I was so mad, I felt like flying out of bed
and demanding to know where she'd been.
I'd been worrying about her like a mother,
imagining all sorts of terrible things. Car
accidents, muggings, abduction. How could
she have done this to me? She wasn't the

one who had to play tennis in the morning. She had another day to prepare. But I had to be on the warm-up court in six hours, match play in eight. I couldn't afford to waste precious sleep worrying about her.

I flopped onto my side and closed my eyes. The water shut off in the bathroom. Within seconds the door opened, and light spilled into the room. I pretended to be asleep. I didn't want to get into it with her now. It would just rile me up more, and then I'd never sleep.

She snapped the light off and crept across the room to sit on her bed, less than a meter away from me. She'd been drinking. I could smell it on her.

"Kat?" she whispered. "You awake?"

Stubbornly, I kept my eyes shut tight. Whatever she wanted to talk about, it could wait until morning. Let her stew on it for a bit.

She crawled between the sheets, and a short time later I heard her snoring. I lay staring at the wall. Wide awake.

She slept through the alarm the next morning. When I came out of the shower, she was out cold.

"Go away," she said when I shook her awake.

"Get up," I said. "We're due on the courts in half an hour."

She pulled the sheet over her head. "I'm not playing today," she said. "My head hurts."

"Well, it serves you right," I said. "What were you doing partying before a tournament? Hugo will kill you."

Her hand snaked out and grabbed my wrist. She flung the sheet off her face.

"He doesn't know I was out last night, does he?" she said furiously.

I threw her hand off and glared at her. "No, he doesn't," I said. "But I don't know why I bothered to cover for you. Where were you, anyway?"

She ignored the question. "Kat, he can't find out about this. You can't tell him. He'll make me withdraw. Promise me you won't tell."

I shook my head in disgust. "Only because I need you for the doubles," I said. "But you have to get up. If you blow this for me, Miri..."

She lay back in the bed and covered her eyes with her arm. "Don't freak out," she said. "It's just qualifiers."

I didn't say anything. I couldn't. I thought if I tried, I might strangle her.

She sighed. "All right. You go. I'll be there in a bit."

I was halfway through my warm-up when Miri finally showed. I didn't hear what she said to Hugo, but he seemed to accept her explanation. Not that he looked happy about it. They sparred for a couple of minutes while I jogged on the spot, but in the end he allowed her to take his place on the other side of the court. Miri winked at me conspiratorially. Like we were in on it together. I just glared at her.

We started rallying, but she may as well have stayed in bed, the way she was playing.

I'd never seen her move so slowly. As she halfheartedly returned ball after ball, I got madder and madder. This was my final warm-up. I didn't need to be chasing crappy shots. I needed to get my feet moving, get the blood pumping, hit some winners. By seven thirty, I was so wound up that even the easiest forehands were going wild. Hugo called us off the court.

"I don't know what you two were up to last night," he said, "but you both better shape up. I didn't come over here to get eliminated in the first round." He turned to me. "Kat, you've got one hour. I suggest you go somewhere where you can get your head together."

He walked off and left me glaring at Miri. She shrugged. "You heard what he said. Go...meditate or something."

I went for a run.

Back in Vancouver, I used to do cross-country in the off-season. Running always clears my head. The feel of the ground beneath my feet, the rush of air past my face, the pulsing of my heart. It blows the cobwebs out of my brain. So I turned my back on Miri and jogged off the court, through the grounds and out onto the street. Ignoring the morning traffic crawling through the city, I put one foot in front of the other until the anger melted away. The pounding in my head disappeared, and my muscles started to move like they should. I returned to court 12 half an hour later, out of breath but ready to play tennis.

Amelia Barrett arrived with an entourage of supporters. Parents, brothers, grandparents, who all clapped and cheered wildly when she won a point. On my side was dead silence. I went out nervous but mildly confident. She had the disadvantage of being about five foot nothing. She also had an annoying habit of smoothing back her tightly bound chestnut hair before every point. If Hugo thought I could beat her, I probably could.

I quickly discovered he was right about her backhand. It was definitely her weakest stroke. That didn't mean she was a pushover. I had to fight for every point. She was quick on her feet and had an amazing forehand that she could place wherever she wanted on the court. I felt like I was running a marathon.

I was up 5-4 when Hugo, Miri and Hamish showed up. After my run that morning, the long rallies were starting to take their toll. I knew I had to mix it up a bit. I couldn't afford to let her run me around like she had been.

I bounced the ball a couple of times, buying a bit of time. Squinting at Amelia on the other side of the court, I saw she was positioned close to the center line, so she could take the serve on her forehand. Well, fine. If she wanted a forehand, I'd give it to her. Adjusting my grip on the racket, I tossed the ball up, brought the racket around and sliced the serve wide.

She dived for it, but at little over five feet tall, her reach was pretty short. The ball tipped the end of the racket and kept going.

A groan from the entourage. Silence from Hugo and company.

"Fifteen-love," I said.

I sent my next serve onto her backhand. A power serve that I thought would be an ace, but she got her racket out and the ball ricocheted back over the net. It landed a meter inside the baseline. I could have hit it with a forehand. It was a fairly easy shot. But that would have got the rally going again, and the last thing I needed was another marathon. Instead, I lobbed it high and deep. She shuffled back, waiting for it to bounce. The ball landed just where I wanted it to, almost on the baseline, and bounced high over her head. She leapt up and swung at it, but she was just too short to make contact.

"Thirty-love."

There was a muttering from Amelia Barrett's family. They didn't like my tactics, but I didn't care. I would do whatever it took to win.

I moved over to the forehand court and served the next one up straight away. I sent it out wide again, hoping she was still protecting her backhand side. This time she was ready for it. She shuffled to the right and returned the serve with a strong forehand. There was good topspin on it, and it accelerated off the bounce. I sliced it back down the line. It dropped low with a bit of backspin, and I thought I had her. But somehow she managed to scoop it up and tip it over the net. I dashed in, racket stretched out, and missed it by millimeters.

A huge cheer went up. The clapping seemed to go on and on.

I glanced over at Hugo. His face was as unreadable as ever. Miri and Hamish looked bored.

"Thirty-fifteen," I said.

I bounced the ball, waiting for the noise to die down. But this wasn't Wimbledon, and there was no umpire to caution the excited family supporters of Amelia Barrett. Finally I tossed the ball up for the serve anyway. It wasn't the best toss, and I hit it a bit flat. The serve went long.

"Fault!" called Amelia.

I cursed under my breath. *Come on, Kat. Just finish this.*

I put the second serve in short. Amelia shuffled in and hit it with her forehand, then ran in to the net. Not a good idea when you're five foot nothing. I lobbed it over her head. She ran back, but there wasn't much she could do.

"Forty–fifteen."

Okay. Match point. If I won this one, I was a step closer to qualifying for the tournament. No pressure.

I served it onto her backhand. She returned it down the line, low and flat. A quick two-step and a powerful forehand crosscourt sent her racing for the shot. Somehow she managed to get there and sent it back again with a matching forehand. The rally was on. Quickly I shuffled to the right and hit it down the line. Again she got her racket on it. She wasn't going down easy. The backhand landed on the service line, and I ran in, tapping it over with a quick backhand slice, then following it to the net. I could only hope she wouldn't lob it over my head like I had done to her.

She shuffled in to the shot. It had landed on her backhand side. She turned for the backswing and brought her racket around. I think it was meant to go over my head. I saw her gaze move in that direction, but I was a lot taller than her, and backhand was not her best stroke. The ball came straight at my head. Luckily, my reflexes had been honed by training with Miri. I'd lost count of the number of times she'd fired body shots at me. I got the racket up and deflected the ball to the left.

I saw Amelia staring at the spot on the court where the ball had landed, almost on the sideline. She couldn't possibly be thinking of calling it out, could she? She glanced up at her family, then back at me. She pressed her lips together.

"Good game," she muttered as we shook hands.

"Yeah, good game," I said. I was leaping up and down inside.

I turned toward Hugo, who nodded approvingly. Hamish and Miri were nowhere to be seen.

chapter four

"You looked tired out there" was all Hugo said when I joined him courtside.

"Yeah, we had some long rallies in the first half," I said. I didn't mention the half-hour run through the streets of Melbourne. Somehow I didn't think that was high on the list of recommended preparation exercises on the day of a tournament.

"Make sure you rest up before your next match," he said. He pulled an energy bar out of his pack. "Here. Have one of these a half an hour before you play. It'll keep you going."

"Thanks," I said.

He turned to go. "Oh, and by the way. Amelia Barrett was meant to win that one."

"What?" I glanced over to the other side of the court, where Amelia's family was gathered around her.

"She won this tournament last year in the 14 and Under," he said. "She's only in the qualifiers because she's been off with an ankle injury." He nodded toward two guys who had taken over the court and were rallying back and forth. "Both her brothers play as well. Mark, the oldest, is one of the best juniors in the country, and Colby is no slouch either. He'll give Hamish a run for his money this weekend."

The boys were both tall, unlike Amelia, who must have got her height—or lack of it—from her mother. One of the boys had longish dark hair tied back off his face. He looked a lot like his dad, who I'd spotted earlier cheering on Amelia. I figured this boy was probably Mark, the oldest. The other one looked more like his sister, with short chestnut hair and freckles. They both had amazing technique, I could tell, even though they were just fooling around.

"But you told me last night Amelia was nothing to worry about. That I'd beat her," I said to Hugo.

"And you did, didn't you?" he said.

I looked back at Hugo. He didn't usually play games. Then again, I'd only been training with him for a month. What did I know?

"Look, Kat," he said. "I wouldn't have brought you if I thought you couldn't do it. It was a tough draw. I didn't want you to psych yourself out. Now your next one should be a breeze. You play the winner from court 8. Go and see what's happening, and be ready to play again at eleven thirty."

I hurried over to court 8. The match had gone to a tiebreak. The two girls were pretty evenly matched and also fairly average, from what I could see. The taller girl had strong strokes but was a bit slow, so missed the shots that went close to the line. The other girl, who was about my height, was quicker but not very consistent. She made a lot of unforced errors. I thought I could probably beat either one.

The match was over quickly. I figured the shorter girl gave up in the end. Once the taller girl broke her serve, she didn't win another point. That was all right with me. I'd gotten enough of a look at my next opponent to be prepared, and besides, my stomach was raging at me. I'd been too mad at Miri to eat anything but a Mars bar for breakfast. I needed food.

For an athletic competition, there was an awful lot of junk food on offer. Burgers, hot dogs, grilled sandwiches...and it all smelled good. I admit I was tempted. I hadn't eaten a French fry or potato chip or even had a soft drink in over a week, which was kind of a record for me. I knew junk food wasn't a good idea, though, and settled on a banana smoothie. I only hoped it wouldn't still be sloshing around in my stomach when it was time to play.

Drink in hand, I turned around and almost bumped into Miri. She was with a blond guy who looked a bit older than us, about seventeen or eighteen, though he wasn't much taller than she was. His skin was tanned to a golden brown, and he looked totally full of himself. He gave me the creeps.

I went to walk past them, but Miri caught my arm. "Kat, wait up," she said.

The guy looked me up and down, and then his gaze slid away. Like slime sliding off a rock. "I'll catch you later," he said to Miri.

"Who was that?" I asked when he'd left.

"Him?" she said. "Dray Yule. He trains with Mark deLany—although, between you and me, I don't know why he took him on. He's not really that good."

The trainer's name didn't mean anything to me, but the way Miri had thrown it out, I thought he must be one of the better trainers around. I glanced back and saw that Dray had stopped to talk to someone, but his eyes were still on us. I didn't want to guess what he was thinking.

"Do you know him?" I asked.

Miri shrugged. "I've seen him around. He's always at the Melbourne tournaments. It's his home town. By the way, I hear you won," she said. "Congrats. When I saw you were playing Amelia Barrett, I thought you were a goner."

"Thanks for the vote of confidence," I said, remembering suddenly what she'd done that morning. I started to walk away, but she turned and kept pace with me, pulling her cell phone out and scrolling through the menu.

"We've got an easy draw tomorrow morning," she said. "The Wong sisters. They're nothing special. Maddy and I have played them a few times." She chatted on about them as we walked. As if nothing had happened the night before. As if we were friends.

Finally, I stopped and faced her. "Miri, what do you want?" I said. "In case you're wondering, I'm still mad about last night. And no, I don't want to talk about it. I've got to play soon."

She rolled her eyes. "There's no pleasing you. I try to be nice and you bite my head off."

"It's a bit late for nice, don't you think?" I said.

She scowled. "Okay, okay! I'm sorry about last night. If it makes you feel any better, Hugo's put me on notice for being late this morning."

She actually did look sorry. Whether it was for screwing me around or getting in hot water with Hugo, I'd never know. I could only hope it was a bit of both.

I sighed. "Look, Miri," I said. "All I want is to play tennis. The fact is that we have to play doubles together, and that's going to be a whole lot easier if we're not at each other's throats. So why don't we start over. Forget about last night and concentrate on our game."

Her face brightened. "Exactly what I was thinking."

I took a sip of my smoothie. "So what about these Wong sisters?" I said.

"Don't worry about them," she said, dismissing them with a wave of her hand.

"If you can beat Amelia Barrett, you can beat Leah and Nora Wong." Her phone bleeped, and she glanced at a text that had just come in. "I've gotta go. But Kat, can I ask one teensie favor?"

I should have known it was too good to be true. "As long as it doesn't involve lying to Hugo," I said.

"No, nothing like that." She looked over her shoulder toward the change rooms. "I promised Hamish I would pick up his spare racket from the restring service, but it won't be ready until eleven and I've gotta meet someone. Could you...?"

"But...I have to be on the court at eleven thirty," I protested.

"It won't take long." Her phone bleeped again, and she started backing away. "Hamish is on the warm-up courts with Hugo. I owe you one." She dashed off toward the change rooms, and I was left standing there with a melted smoothie, realizing I'd been duped again.

chapter five

Hamish wasn't surprised when I showed up with his racket, which made me wonder whether Miri had planned to make me her errand boy all along.

"Hey, I meant to tell you congrats on your win this morning," he said. His eyes were a deep blue. I'd never noticed that before. "I was watching you play. You're not bad. Not bad at all."

I knew it was a compliment. His smile was warm and genuine.

"Thanks." I grinned stupidly.

"Don't you have somewhere to be?" asked Hugo from behind me.

I jumped guiltily. "Yeah, I'm going," I said. "Wish me luck."

"Luck has nothing to do with it," said Hugo. "Get out there and play tennis."

"Good luck!" said Hamish as I ran off.

The tall girl was waiting for me. She wasn't actually that tall, not as tall as Miri anyway, but that was how I thought of her. Her name was Emily Hunt. She was from Sydney and had arrived in Melbourne the day before, on the same flight as us. She recognized me from the line at the baggage carousel. This was also her first time playing at Melbourne Park. She seemed excited that we had so much in common—and nervous too. Like she needed to tell me her life story before we got started. I was pleased to see she didn't have a cheer squad with her.

We headed out on the court to warm up, and I reviewed my plan for the match. It was pretty simple, really. Move her around and make her run for the ball. She had lead feet. If I placed my shots well, I could tire her out and force her to make mistakes.

It was all going according to plan. I got the feeling she was already pretty tired from the first match, so it didn't take much to wear her out. She didn't have the energy to chase after difficult shots. I was up 4–1 when things took a turn for the worse.

We stopped to change ends, and the world started spinning.

"Are you all right?" she said.

"I'm fine," I said. "I just need a minute."

I sat at the edge of the court and put my head on my knees. I could hear the blood pumping through my veins. My stomach was a hollow pit.

I felt a hand on my back, and a bottle of Powerade was thrust under my nose.

"Here, drink this," said Hamish.

"Did you eat that bar I gave you?" said Hugo, squatting on my other side.

I took a sip of the drink and shook my head. I hadn't had much of the smoothie either. He swore.

"Have one of mine," said Hamish. "I can get some more."

My hands were shaking as I ripped open the packet. The bar was fruity and sweet, and I felt the sugar going straight to my energy-starved body. I ate the whole thing in three bites.

A shadow blocked the sun, and I looked up to see Emily standing over me. "Is she all right?" she said. "Does she need to forfeit?" I could hear the eagerness in her voice, though to be fair, she was trying to look concerned. I couldn't blame her. If I forfeited, she'd move on to the next round.

"No," I said. "I'm all right. I was just a bit dizzy for a second."

I stood up. The world tilted and then evened out. I took another sip of the Powerade and a swig of water.

"All set," I said, hoping I was. "Let's play."

It was Emily's serve. She tightened her ponytail and adjusted her cap, then glanced at the sun, which was right overhead. I didn't mind. The longer she took, the longer I had to recover. I wasn't dizzy anymore, but I felt heavy and sluggish, like I had weights attached to my wrists and ankles.

She tossed the ball up for the serve, and I went up on my toes, ready for the return. Her racket arced up and around. The ball rocketed toward me. I shuffled in just as it slammed into the net.

Whew. Saved by a fault. The way I was feeling, it probably would have been an ace if it had gone over.

Her next serve was slow and easy. I shuffled around to take it on my forehand, going for a power shot crosscourt. Only there was no power there. I managed to get a bit of topspin on it, but there was no acceleration, and the ball plopped softly into the court just past the service line. Emily lined it up and powered it down the line in a passing shot that should never have happened.

I couldn't believe it. It was an easy shot. I should have got to it. I would have got to it, if I had half the get-up-and-go I usually had. But it was like there was a half-second delay in messages getting from my brain to my feet. The next two points were just as bad. I tried to hit them deep, and they landed well inside the baseline, setting her up for a clean winner. I was in real trouble. I had to do something. I wasn't sure exactly what, but anything would be better than what I was doing now. I'd missed three points in a row, and at 40–love I had little to lose.

She sent the next serve straight toward me. I sidestepped and took it on the forehand, lobbing it high and hoping she didn't have a great smash hidden up her sleeve. She didn't. She scooted backward and lobbed it back at me, nice and deep. I lobbed it back again to her backhand side. With plenty of time, she moved around to take it on her forehand. Now I had her where I wanted her. Deep in the corner on the backhand side. I moved forward to take the shot early and angled it short on her forehand side. I didn't need power for that, just accuracy. She watched helplessly as it landed well inside the line but far out of her reach.

"Great shot, Kat," called Hamish. I glanced over and he grinned at me, giving me a thumbs-up with both hands.

I smiled to myself as I moved back into position. It felt good to have someone cheering me on. Not just anyone, but someone who knew a lot about tennis and would know a good shot when he saw one.

Next thing I knew, Emily had served and the ball powered straight past me. So much for my comeback.

I was feeling a bit better now though. The energy bar and the Powerade were kicking in. I had a strategy. Move her around and keep her guessing. Try to keep the points short. I couldn't afford to get into long rallies. It was Amelia Barrett all over again.

I served the first ball short and wide, just like she'd done to me. She managed to get her racket on it, but it landed out.

Okay. Back on track. Fifteen–love.

She returned the next serve with interest, which wasn't hard. My serves weren't what they should be. It landed deep, and I blocked it back. The ball flew high over the net.

I watched her move in for the kill. She did have a smash after all. Her timing was perfect, her racket arcing down over the ball just at the right moment. It slammed into the middle of the service court and bounced over my head.

Fifteen all.

I won the next two points through sheer determination, stubbornly moving her back side to side and then popping in a short shot. I thought my plan was working. She was breathing hard, taking her time getting back into position to receive the ball. It was taking its toll on me too, though. Those rallies had been way too long. I was tiring. Fast.

Forty–15. One more point, and I'd be up 5–2 and one game away from taking the match and qualifying for the main tournament. Hugo and Hamish were still watching from the sidelines. I snuck a peek at them as I bounced the ball. Hugo looked grim, Hamish worried.

I tossed the ball up and sliced it out wide. Emily took two quick steps, stretched and blocked it back. The ball arced toward the net, hit the tape and tipped onto my side of the court. I groaned. Luck was on her side.

She seemed to know it too. I faulted on the next serve and had to lob in an easy second. Suddenly the tables were turned. It was her advantage, and I had no idea how it had happened.

I bounced the ball, trying to think. I needed something special now. I couldn't afford to fault on my first serve. She was positioned far into the forehand court. Waiting for the slice, maybe?

I took a deep breath, tossed the ball up and slammed it down the center line. She seemed to have her second wind though. She pivoted around and returned it with a flat backhand that skimmed the top of the net and kept coming. I ducked to the side but couldn't get my racket around. The ball nicked the rim and flew on past me.

Her game.

There was no containing her excitement. She'd broken my serve, and it was the turning point for the match. Her shots started coming harder and faster. She moved more quickly. I'd pop in a drop shot, and she'd get in and drop it back over the net again.

I didn't make it easy for her. I fought long and hard, but in the end the score was 7-5 and that was it. My chance to compete in the singles was over.

chapter six

I don't know who was more disappointed in me, Hugo or myself. I knew I'd blown it. I could have won that match. Correction. I *should* have won that match. And would have, easily, if it weren't for stupid mistakes. Like getting no sleep and then exhausting myself running errands for Miri between matches. And forgetting to eat. I mean, that was pretty basic, wasn't it? Food equals energy?

"Bad luck," said Hamish.

But Hugo was right. Luck had nothing to do with it.

"I'm sorry," I said to Hugo. "It won't happen again."

"See that it doesn't," he said. He didn't need to say anything else about the loss. It was written all over his face. "Carbs tonight. Lots of them, and a light meal in the morning. Have a sports drink or an energy bar on hand at all matches. This is basic stuff, Kat. I didn't think I needed to spell it out."

"Yeah, sorry," I said. I felt about five years old.

"Now forget about it and concentrate on the doubles."

He and Hamish headed back to the warm-up courts, and I was left to wallow in my misery. The sound of balls on rackets was suddenly extremely irritating. Everywhere I looked, someone was serving an ace or smashing a winner down the line or racing in for a tricky volley. No one was sitting with their head between their knees, fighting to stay conscious. It's not like it was forty degrees and I'd been overcome by the heat or anything. It was just stupid mistakes, pure and simple.

I turned away and headed back to the hotel. I needed to eat, but I could get something at the café next door. I couldn't stand watching these superstars play when I'd ruined it for myself so completely.

After a chicken-and-veggie wrap, I did feel microscopically better. If not on cloud nine, at least a bit more like myself. I even thought I might go back to Melbourne Park and seek out the Wong sisters so I could have a look at their game. Miri seemed a bit too sure of herself for my liking. And if I wanted to get back into Hugo's good books, there was only one way to redeem myself.

As I swallowed the last of my wrap, I glanced out the window and saw Miri leaving the hotel. She'd changed into jeans and a jacket and had her purse slung over her shoulder. She darted a quick look down the street toward the café, then headed the other way, moving fast. I grabbed my tennis bag and dashed out to catch her. Expecting her to cross the road and head toward the tennis complex, I was surprised to see her round the corner and disappear. I hesitated for only a split second before following her.

I stayed a fair distance back so she wouldn't notice me as we headed up Jolimont Road toward the center of the city. It was a busy street, four lanes of traffic whizzing past at sixty kilometers an hour, but there wasn't much foot traffic. She glanced back once, about halfway up the hill, and I ducked into a shop doorway, hoping she hadn't seen me. When I peeked out, I thought I'd lost her. Then I spotted her standing on an island in the middle of the road at a tram stop. She hopped onto the first tram that came by, one of the free City Circle tourist trams, an old-fashioned wooden car that clanked and clunked its way down the road before squealing to a stop. I dashed across and hopped on the back of it.

Luckily, the tram was quite full. I was able to slouch in a seat at the back where Miri couldn't see me. The tram rocked and wheezed its way up the street toward the city center. After ten minutes or so, Miri pulled the bell for the next stop. As she was making her way through the people standing in the aisle, I ducked out the back and slid into the crowd on the sidewalk.

We were at a busy intersection, with masses of people around. They shoved past me, heads down, intent on their business. Many of them were talking on cell phones or texting as they walked. I looked up and saw an old stone building with arched entrances and a domed top. The sign above the entry said *Flinders Street Station*.

Miri had a quick look around and then ran up the steps in front of the station. I followed her as she disappeared through the archway. Finding a small flower shop just inside, I hid behind a stand of daffodils and peered out to see what she was doing.

She stopped in front of the ticket machine and glanced around, as if she was looking for someone or something. Not finding who or what she was looking for, she pulled out her phone and checked it, then pocketed it again. She stood staring at the map of the city rail system, glancing over her shoulder every so often. People came and bought tickets, stood next to her to check the map and brushed past to move through the turnstile, but she just stood and waited. She looked nervous.

The lady who owned the flower shop was starting to glare at me when someone sidled up behind Miri, leaned in close and whispered something in her ear.

Miri jumped as if she'd been stung. She turned toward the newcomer, taking a step back. As he moved closer, I recognized the blond hair and tanned skin of Dray Yule, the guy she'd been talking to earlier. I wasn't close enough to hear them, but Miri didn't look happy. I'd seen that look on her face often enough to recognize it with my eyes closed. They talked for no more than two minutes, and then Miri handed something to Dray. He pocketed it before I could get a look at it. Without another word, he slunk into the crowd.

chapter seven

"Are you going to buy something, love?" The shopkeeper's voice startled me out of my trance. "'Cause if you're not, I'd appreciate it if you'd move on."

I smiled apologetically and backed away from the flower shop. Miri was gone. I didn't know what I was going to do when I saw her again. I couldn't let her know I'd followed her. She'd kill me. But I had a bad feeling about what I'd seen.

Dray Yule was bad news. I knew that the first time I laid eyes on him. And Miri didn't want anyone to know she'd met up with him. Otherwise, they would have met at the tennis courts. That meant she knew they were doing something wrong. Or was it just that she didn't want Hamish to see her with him? That he might think she was cheating on him? I didn't think so. They had met at the station so she could give Dray the package. But what was in it? Money? Drugs? I didn't think Miri was into that stuff. She was so conscious about what she put in her body. So serious about her tennis. At least, I'd thought she was. Until last night. What did I really know about Miri, anyway? Nothing. She was my tennis partner. She could hit a ball and do a damn good job of it. That's all I knew. What I also knew now was that she was involved in some kind of intrigue with Dray Yule.

By the time I'd made it back to Melbourne Park, all the matches were over, so it was too late to scope out the Wong sisters.

Miri was in the room when I got there. She'd changed again and was dressed for going out.

"Where have you been?" she said.

I was tempted to say Flinders Street Station, just to see what she would do. But I didn't. "Just getting something to eat," I said.

"That's good," said Miri, tying a scarf around her neck. "Hamish and I are going out and, no offense, you're not invited."

"No worries." I dropped my tennis bag on the bed. She was acting so normal. You'd never have thought she'd been having a clandestine meeting at a city train station only an hour ago.

"Hugo was looking for you."

"Oh?" I paused, one shoe off and one shoe on. "Was it important?"

"Nah, he said he'd catch up with you at curfew." She winked. "Assuming you're back."

"Ha ha," I said.

There was a knock on the door.

"That'll be Hamish," she said. "Do you want to let him in? I still need to do my hair."

I couldn't see anything wrong with it myself, but she disappeared into the bathroom, so I got up and opened the door.

"Hey, Kat," Hamish said. I'd heard people talk about infectious smiles. His really was. I grinned back at him. "Miri ready?"

"Not yet." I let him in. There was an awkward pause as we stood there waiting for Miri. "Ready for tomorrow?" I asked.

"Ready as I'll ever be," he said. "What about you? You feeling better? Ready for the doubles?"

I flushed, recalling that he'd seen my embarrassing loss earlier. "Yeah."

"Don't worry about this afternoon. We all make stupid mistakes," he said. With a glance at the bathroom door, he leaned toward me and dropped his voice. "The first time Miri came to Melbourne Park, she loaded up on so much junk food the night before that she could hardly lift her racket. Got skunked in the first round." He laughed.

I laughed too, but inside I was thinking, Miri and junk food? It was hard to believe.

Miri came out of the bathroom. Talk about bad timing.

"What are you two talking about?" she said suspiciously. "Kat, you're as red as a tomato."

"Nothing," I said, feeling myself go even redder.

Hamish jumped in before she could give me the third degree. "I was just telling her about my first tournament at Melbourne Park."

"When you got in that fight with Colby Barrett and got disqualified in the semifinal?" Miri smirked. "You were what, twelve, thirteen?"

"Uh—yeah." Hamish looked a little red himself now.

"Isn't Colby Barrett Amelia's brother?" I said, trying to steer the conversation away from what we'd actually been talking about. "I heard he's pretty good."

"He is," said Hamish. "Really good. In fact, if he wins this weekend, he's going to take the number-one ranking for 16 and Under."

"And if you win, you'll be number one," said Miri.

"Well, yeah, there's that," said Hamish with a grin.

"So what stupid thing did you do today to get Hamish talking about ancient history?" Miri asked.

I told her, and her jaw dropped. "In the qualifier? You didn't even make it into the tournament?"

By this time, I knew my face must be glowing like Rudolph's nose. "Let's not talk about it, all right? Aren't you going out or something?"

Miri slung her purse over her shoulder and grabbed her jacket and phone. "You pull something like that tomorrow, and you're dead."

My jaw dropped. She'd had as much hand in my loss as I had—the late night, the running around, the poor practice session. If I hadn't needed her for the doubles, I would have let the accusations fly. "Whatever," I said.

Hamish rolled his eyes at me behind Miri's back. I bit back a grin as they went out the door.

chapter eight

When we arrived at the warm-up courts the next morning, I could see right away that Hamish was in a bad mood. I wondered if something had happened between him and Miri the night before. From the look of it, they'd had a pretty quiet night. Miri was back well before curfew, and there'd been no smell of alcohol on her. She'd seemed tense though. Quiet. I'd put it down to pre-tournament jitters. Even the pros get them, right? But now, with Hamish acting strangely too...All the drama was giving me a headache.

Hugo put us through our drills, and I forgot about the lovebirds. We were up against the Wong sisters at eight thirty. He set us up with some extra volley practice, which made me wonder if they were really good at the net. Or maybe it meant they weren't good at the net at all, and if we took the offense, we'd intimidate them and put them off their game. I just had no idea. I wished I'd had a chance to check them out the day before.

It turned out the Wong sisters were twins. A matching pair with blue tennis skirts, black ponytails, white visors, and braces on their eager smiles. Not only were they twins, they were mirror-image twins—identical except for the fact that one was right-handed and the other left-handed. I didn't know which one was Leah and which one was Nora. I didn't suppose it mattered. Someone might have warned me about the mirror-twin bit, though, before we rocked up to the courts at eight twenty and started hitting. No one seemed to have thought it was important enough to mention.

Left-handers are hard to beat. Their forehand is on the backhand side, they slice out wide on the serve, and their spin goes the opposite direction from what you expect. Playing a left-hander paired with a right-handed twin seemed like a double whammy.

Miri was altogether too relaxed about the whole thing for my liking. She hit through the first game like it was a Sunday-afternoon social match, lobbing easy forehands back to them, backhanding the ball crosscourt to the left-hander's forehand, hitting easy shots to the player at the net. Okay, I had to admit they weren't the strongest of players. They were small, and they didn't hit particularly hard or fast, but they were quick on their feet, and they had both the left-hander and the twin advantages. I wasn't going to make the mistake of underestimating them.

It was 40–30 our way when Miri let a volley pass her by. I chased it down but couldn't reach it in time. That made the score deuce instead of game.

I glared at Miri, but she just shrugged. Like it didn't matter to her whether we won the match or not.

Either Leah or Nora served the ball down the middle. Not very hard, but right on the line. Miri took it with her backhand and hit it straight back to center court. Straight into the forehand of both girls. She couldn't have set them up better if she'd tried. Luckily, instead of shooting a winner down the line like she should have, the right-hander volleyed it into my court. I blocked it back short, leaving the left-hander racing for the net. She scooped it up, but it dropped back onto her side.

Miri was oblivious to the whole thing. I didn't know where her brain was, but it sure wasn't on the court, playing doubles with me.

I stood out near the tramline, anticipating a slice serve from the left-hander. It came exactly where I'd expected, and I shuffled across to take it on my backhand.

With the ball out wide, there was nothing to do but send it down the line and hope that the girl at the net wasn't on the ball. No such luck. She stepped across and volleyed it back into the middle of the service court. Miri should have got it. Any other day she would have, but today she gave it a halfhearted swipe that missed completely. I dashed toward the net, caught it on my forehand and lobbed it over the right-hander's head. Her sister moved quickly into the deuce court and tried to take it with her backhand. It was an awkward stretch for the left-hander, and it didn't make the distance.

Game.

"What's with you?" I said to Miri as we changed ends.

"I know, I should have got that," she said, totally un-Miri-like. Something was seriously wrong.

"Yeah, you should have. You're playing like crap," I said.

Miri's jaw clenched at the insult. "It's not like we're playing the Williams sisters, you know," she whispered with a glance toward the other girls. "We still won the game."

"No thanks to you," I said. "Whatever's bugging you, forget about it until after the match. I want to win this one."

Miri's eyes flashed with anger. I didn't care. Whatever it took to get her playing. "We will," she said. "Stop being such a worrywart."

It was our serve. Miri stepped up to the baseline, bounced the ball a couple of times like she always does, then fired an ace down the center line.

She arched her eyebrows at me. "Happy?"

"Yeah," I said.

She served the next one out wide and deep. Unfortunately, it was to the left-hander. On her forehand side. The girl shuffled over and sent it back down the tramline with a topspin forehand. I stretched across and volleyed it back, but it flew wide and landed out.

"Fifteen all," said Miri. I could hear the annoyance in her voice. Like it was my fault.

I turned and pointed to my left hand. Meaning, pay attention to the left-hander. Miri barely glanced at me.

Her next serve landed wide.

"Fault!" called a Wong sister. I still didn't know which one.

Miri popped in a second serve, short and close to the center line. The right-hander moved in and hit it on her backhand down the middle. I leapt across for a forehand volley and tapped it back, aiming for the left-hander's backhand. She was good at the net though. She volleyed it back again, straight at Miri. Miri leapt aside, caught it with an inside-out forehand and lobbed it high over the net. Without missing a beat, the twins switched sides. The right-hander waited behind the baseline for it to land.

"Out!" she called.

The Wong sisters high-fived each other, and I glared at Miri. This was my only chance at competing in this tournament. If she blew it because of a stupid fight with Hamish...

Miri bounced the ball. Then bounced it again. She threw the ball up, brought her racket around and smashed the ball down the center line. The Wong sister didn't even have time to flinch.

And so it went. Miri was hot and cold. She'd mess up easy shots and then pull out a winner at the most unexpected time.

The score was deuce. Then our ad. Then deuce again. Their ad, and deuce again. We went back and forth through I don't know how many deuces until Miri started getting mad. And when Miri gets mad, she gets wild. She wound up and let fly with a flat forehand that rocketed across the net at about 150 k's, flew between the two Wong sisters and hit the backstop. It was their game. They stared at her with twin sets of eyes drawn so wide, I could see the whites even from my side of the court.

"Get a grip," I whispered furiously to Miri.

Miri's shoulders rose and fell as she breathed deeply, adjusting the strings on her racket. Slowly she walked back to the baseline. When she turned around, her face was calm, her jaw set. I smiled grimly.

I'd seen that look before and been on the other end of it many times. And just like that, we were back in business. The Wong sisters only won one more game.

"What's your hurry?" I said as we packed up our stuff.

Miri already had her bag slung over her shoulder. She glanced at her phone. "Hamish started his match at nine thirty, and I promised I'd be there."

I jogged after her as she hurried off toward the other end of the courts. "I thought you guys had a fight."

"No, why did you think that?" She looked genuinely surprised.

"You were back so early last night, and Hamish was in such a bad mood, I just figured you must have argued or something." I shrugged.

"Well, we didn't," said Miri. She grinned. "Quite the opposite, in fact."

I didn't want to know what she meant by that. "So what's up with Hamish?"

"He lost his medallion," she said. "His mother gave it to him, and he always wears it when he plays. It's sort of a good-luck charm."

I'd heard of tennis players who were like that, having superstitions and set routines they followed before a match. Did it really matter that much? "Does he think he can't win without it or something?"

Miri shrugged. "It's important to him. He doesn't see his mom much anymore."

That made me curious, but there was no time to ask any more questions. We'd arrived at court 1, where Hamish was playing his first singles match. He didn't look like he'd just lost his good-luck charm. In fact, he looked more like he was out to prove something. He was hitting hard and strong and fast, jumping at every opportunity, going for the winners. An ace here, then a winner down the line, an overhead smash...I don't think his opponent knew what hit him. It was all over within half an hour. Final score, 6–1.

The win didn't seem to improve Hamish's mood any. In fact, he seemed to take it as a personal insult that the guy had gotten even one game off him. He rummaged through his tennis bag, a scowl on his face, and finally threw it down in disgust.

"I'm out of energy bars," he said, running his hand through his hair. "Can't anything go right today?"

"I'll go get you some," I volunteered. He'd probably given me his last one the day before.

He glanced at me like I was a mosquito to be swatted away. Then he sighed. "Would you? I've got doubles at eleven thirty, and I've got to go back to the hotel first."

To search for his medallion, I was sure. "No worries," I said. "The fruit ones, right?"

"Yeah. Go to Fresh. They always have them."

Fresh didn't have them. And neither did the canteen or the pro shop, although there was an empty box next to the energy bars Hugo liked. They must have had some earlier. I bought a couple of Hugo's brand and made it back to the court just as Hamish was warming up with his doubles partner. Theo Pappas competed in the

14 and Under Singles but was almost as tall as Hamish and had one of the best forehands I'd ever seen. They'd make an intimidating pair.

"They were out of fruit bars," I said, offering Hamish the ones I'd bought.

He swore under his breath. "I can't eat those. I'm allergic to nuts," he said.

I was such an idiot. Miri had told me on the flight over that he was allergic to nuts. Like, deadly allergic. And there it was, stated clearly on the label. *Contains nuts.* "Sorry, Hamish. I'll find some of the others," I said. "There must be a store close by that sells them."

"Forget it," he said. "I've got to go on."

"Did he find his medallion?" I said to Miri as the match started.

"No," she said. "I don't think he'll ever find it." She seemed very matter-of-fact, and it made me wonder why she was so sure.

chapter nine

With a couple of hours before I had to play again, I decided to go off and seek out Hamish's energy bars. But first I needed to get rid of my tennis bag. I was sick of lugging it around everywhere.

I'd just popped the lock on my locker when I heard voices coming from the direction of the boys' change room. I was curious. The voices were intense, on the verge of breaking into an all-out argument. Then I caught the name Hamish Brown, and my ears really perked up. I stashed my bag in the locker and crept closer.

"We had an agreement," the first guy said, his voice low and furious. It sounded vaguely familiar. "This isn't half of what you promised."

"And our little enterprise hasn't worked half as well as you thought," said the other. His voice was deeper, more controlled.

"So he made it through the first round. You didn't expect him to lose to Spencer Parkin, did you?"

"No, but six to one?" A snort of disgust. "He couldn't have played better if you'd given him some kind of performance enhancer. Look. As far as I can see, your idea sucks. Show me some results, then we'll talk payment."

"You'll see results, all right," said the first voice, calmer now. Confident. "Just give it some time to kick in."

The deeper voice grunted. "You'd better hope it doesn't take too long. It's only a three-day tournament."

Then I heard feet moving, and I ducked back into the girls' change room. My heart was pounding like mad. They were up to something. And it involved Hamish. Peering through the door, I saw someone leaving the boys' change room. I didn't recognize him at first, not until he paused to glance around just outside the door. Without thinking, I grabbed my cell phone and snapped a picture, and then another as he was walking away. I was pretty sure it was Colby Barrett. But who had he been talking to?

I got my answer a couple of minutes later when Dray Yule came through the door. I'd have recognized that conceited swagger anywhere. Now I really wanted to know what was going on. It couldn't be a coincidence that he'd met secretly with Miri the day before and was having another secret meeting with Colby Barrett today. Was Miri in on whatever they were doing to Hamish? I knew she could be really nasty at times, but I couldn't believe she would do anything to harm Hamish. And that's what it had sounded like. Like they had a plan to take Hamish out of the competition.

I snapped a couple of photos, and then, on impulse, I followed Dray as he rounded the corner and went out onto the grounds. I had to know what he was up to. He moved quickly, winding his way through the courts where matches were being fought at every turn. It wasn't long before I'd figured out where we were going.

A minute later I saw him slip into the stands outside court 6, where Hamish was playing doubles. What was he up to? I went around the other side and squeezed past a few spectators to sit next to Miri and Hugo.

"Did you get them?" asked Miri.

"What?"

"Hamish's energy bars."

I'd completely forgotten about them. "No, I couldn't find any," I said. I leaned forward to peer past her. Dray was slouched in the end seat of the row, arms folded. His cap almost covered his eyes, but still, I didn't like the way he was eyeing Hamish. Like a cat waiting for a bird to drop into range.

"What's the score?" I asked nervously.

"Hamish and Theo are up five to two," said Miri.

"Already?" I turned my eyes toward the game just in time to see Theo hit a backhand winner down the line.

"Hamish and Theo have played doubles together since Hamish was twelve. Theo used to train with Hugo," Miri explained. "Until he moved here to Melbourne last year. He trains with Morgan Freebairn now, but he and Hamish still play doubles together. Look at them. Why wouldn't they?"

I watched as Hamish tossed the ball up and hit a massive serve down the center of the service court. I wished we had the speed clocks going. It looked close to 150 k's an hour to me. The guy on the receiving end blocked the return, no control over where it was going. He just stuck his racket out and hoped the ball would land inbounds. Theo volleyed it back, and the kid's teammate dived toward the net. Not fast enough. The ball slid past, landed in the court behind him and bounced into the backstop. Point to Hamish and Theo.

I glanced toward the end seat. Dray was gone. He'd slipped out while I was watching the game. Scanning the crowd, I spotted him standing near the entrance to the courts, where Hamish's and Theo's tennis bags were sitting. I watched in disbelief as he took a bottle of Powerade out of his bag and exchanged it for the one in Hamish's.

"This is it. Match point," said Miri.

I looked up to see Hamish setting up for another serve. When he came off court, he'd be going for the Powerade. And instead of his own, he'd get the one Dray had planted. And drink whatever Dray had put in it.

"Have you got a Powerade in your bag?" I asked Miri.

"What?"

"A Powerade," I said. "I need one. Now."

She unzipped her bag, and I grabbed the bottle. Hamish and Theo were approaching the net to shake hands with the other players. I pushed past the spectators, jumped down the steps to the ground and sprinted around to the gate just as Hamish and Theo came out.

"Hey, Hamish, good game," I said, a bit out of breath. I shoved the Powerade toward him. "Here. I couldn't find any of your energy bars, so I got you this instead. Sorry about before."

For a second, I thought he might just brush me off. Tell me to get stuffed and go for his own. Then he took the bottle. "Thanks, Kat. Don't worry about it." He cracked it open and took a long drink.

I chewed on my lip as he stowed his racket in his bag. The suspicious bottle of Powerade was still in there. Seeing Miri approaching, I panicked.

"When's your next game?" I asked.

"Not till three."

"Are you going back to the hotel? I could carry your bag for you." I actually blushed. What a stupid thing to say. But I had to do something.

"Uh...no thanks," he said, giving me a strange look and slinging the bag over his own shoulder. He put his arm around Miri as she came up alongside him. "We're going to get some lunch and then Miri's got her singles at one. We'll catch you later."

"Wait!"

They turned and stared at me.

"I forgot. I—I need to talk to Miri. Just for a minute," I added as she scowled at me.

She rolled her eyes, but I dragged her away and led her behind the stands.

"Don't let Hamish drink the Powerade that's in his bag," I said.

She frowned. "What? Why not?"

I hesitated. I was taking a risk. What if she was in on it? I'd be blowing my cover, and Hamish would still be in danger. But she couldn't be, could she? She wouldn't do that. Not to Hamish.

"Kat, what's going on?"

Her eyes flashed with impatience, but with worry too. Worry that her plan had been discovered? Or worry for Hamish?

"Miri?" Hamish called. "Let's go."

There was no other option. I'd just have to trust her.

"Dray Yule switched the Powerade," I said quickly. I could hear Hamish's footsteps approaching. "Don't let him drink it. I'll explain later."

Hamish came around the end of the stands. "What's the big secret?" he said.

"Nothing," said Miri. She threw a glare my way, the kind you'd give to a pesky fly. "Kat's freaking out about our next match. I told her to chill. It's just doubles." She linked arms with Hamish and pulled him away.

I watched them go, hoping desperately that Miri wasn't involved in whatever was going on and would take my warning seriously.

chapter ten

I couldn't stop thinking about the Powerade in Hamish's bag. What had Dray done to it? What had he put in it that would make Hamish lose a match? As soon as I could, I searched out Miri and Hamish at court 5, where Miri was warming up for her singles match.

"Hey," I said to Hamish as I slid into the seat next to him. I glanced down at his bag. The Powerade was gone. Had Miri managed to get it out or had he drunk it?

Either way, there was nothing I could do about it now.

"Hey," said Hamish. He seemed a lot more relaxed than he had that morning. Was that a good thing, or was he on something? He flashed one of his smiles at me, and I smiled back. To my horror, I felt my cheeks start to go pink. Damn that fair, freckled, traitorous skin!

"I was hoping you'd show up. I wanted to ask you if the guys at the restring center said anything about my racket when you picked it up yesterday."

I thought back. They'd given me the racket, all wrapped in plastic, and the order form, but that was it. I shook my head. "No. Why?"

"They got the tension all wrong," said Hamish. "I went to use it in the doubles, and it was strung way too loose. It probably cost us the first game. I double-faulted twice before I got the feel of it." He saw me frowning and added quickly, "Hey, don't worry about it. I'll take it back and get them to do it again. It's no biggie."

It worried *me* though. Was this another of Dray's tricks? Part of the plan he'd said was going to "kick in?" In a tight game, it could have been disastrous. Could have meant the difference between a win and a loss. Which was what Dray wanted. I was pretty sure I still had Hamish's order form somewhere in my hotel room, and made a note to look for it when I got back.

We watched in silence as a coin was tossed and the match started. Miri chose to serve, always a good move for her. Her serve was one of the strongest I'd seen. Not that I'd been around the Australian circuit much, but I knew what it was like to be on the receiving end of one of her power serves, and it was damn hard to get back. As if to prove me right, her first serve of the match was an ace.

Hamish and Hugo were intent on the game, applauding when Miri hit a good shot, groaning when she went for the winner and missed it. Not that that happened very often. Her opponent was quick, but she seemed inexperienced.

In fact, I was sure I'd seen her playing in the qualifying rounds. As I watched, I could see all the stupid mistakes she was making. The kind inexperienced kids make. Like serving to Miri's forehand when it was her best stroke, or running up to the net when she could easily have stayed on the baseline, only to have Miri lob it over her head. It reminded me of the stupid mistakes I'd made the previous day. How I'd had a chance to be playing today and had blown it. The girl was nothing special. If it had been me against her, I probably could have won. I'd played Miri tons of times, and while I rarely won, I made it a contest. This girl was no match for Miri. After forty-five minutes, it was all over. The score was 6–2, and Miri had barely worked up a sweat.

We wandered over to the board to see who we were playing next. Our second round of doubles was scheduled for three, so we wouldn't get a chance to watch Hamish's next match. Running my finger down the sheet, I saw we were playing

Chelsea O'Brien and Emily Hunt, who'd won their first doubles match 7–5.

Emily Hunt! The name jumped out at me when I saw it. She was the girl who'd beaten me in the qualifying round. My chest tightened in anticipation. I would show her how I could really play. Show her that only bad luck and bad judgment on my part had allowed her to be in the singles at all. I wondered if she had won her first round.

She recognized me when we met at the court. She gave me a nervous little smile, then whispered something to her partner. The girl glanced over at me and pulled Emily into a huddle. I didn't care. Whatever strategy they were planning, I knew I could beat Emily Hunt. And no matter how good Chelsea O'Brien might be, I had Miri on my side.

Chelsea served first. She was tall and skinny. Too skinny. My arms were probably bigger than her legs. She had mousy brown hair pulled up into a ponytail on top of her head. It must have bugged the crap out of her, the way it bounced around every time she moved. She flicked it back as she prepared to serve the first ball.

Given her size, I wasn't expecting much. I'd thought her strength must be being quick on her feet, or being deadly accurate in her strokes. But those scrawny arms had a lot of power. She tossed the ball up, and next thing I knew it was streaking toward me like a fireball. With no time for a full backswing, I sliced it back. Unfortunately, it headed straight for Emily. She volleyed it short into my court, and the first point went to them.

I knew then that we had a fight on our hands. Emily Hunt was better at doubles than singles. It didn't matter so much that she wasn't very agile. She didn't have as much court to cover. And Chelsea O'Brien was a powerhouse. All 110 pounds of her was pure muscle. And she knew how to use it. I'd underestimated my opponents yet again and let my guard down. When we lost the first game, I knew we needed a plan.

"What's our strategy with these two?" I asked Miri.

She shrugged. "I've never played either of them before. But it's only the second round. They wouldn't have put one of the real contenders in the same stream as us."

Typical Miri. So sure of herself. So sure of her game. But I didn't believe it for a minute. This wasn't the Australian Open or anything, where they kept the top seeds apart until the quarterfinals. It was only a junior tournament, and a bronze level at that. I doubted they bothered.

"Emily Hunt is a bit slow," I said. "Not the skinny one, but the other girl. I played her yesterday."

Miri squinted at her. "She's the girl that beat you? She doesn't look that good."

"I told you what happened," I snapped. I didn't need yesterday's loss thrown in my face again. "But if we make her run, she'll tire out and start making some unforced errors. She must have played at least two matches already today, maybe three, depending on how she did in the singles."

"All right. It's a plan." There wasn't any high-fiving or anything, but I felt better having a strategy in place.

Miri took the first serve, and we made Emily run. Anytime we could, we avoided Chelsea and fired the ball Emily's way. And she started making unforced errors, just as we expected. In sheer frustration, Chelsea started chasing balls that should have been Emily's. Darting into center court to catch a volley, racing crosscourt to get ones we lobbed over her head, running into the net for a short ball and leaving her side of the court open for a winner. They both knew what was happening. Emily knew she'd been targeted as the weaker player. I could see her shoulders drooping, her racket sliding a little lower. She even started double-faulting on her serve. I felt a bit sorry for her. But this was a competition, and I was there to win, not to do her any favors. I'd already done her a massive favor by messing up my qualifier. I wasn't going to let sympathy drive me into letting her win again. Or even come close.

We couldn't do anything about Chelsea's power service game, though, and Emily managed to hold her serve once too. But when the match ended with a win at 6–4, I was happy. We were still in it, and I'd proved to myself and to Emily Hunt that it should have been me playing the singles today, not her.

"Good game," I said as we shook hands. "How did you do in your singles?"

She looked surprised and a bit embarrassed that I'd asked. "Oh, I lost six to one in the first round," she mumbled.

So she was out of the tournament. I felt sorry for her but a little glad, too, that she'd lost. She should never have gotten through the qualifier. "Bad luck," I said.

A shy smile crossed her face. Again, it was like we were best buddies. "You know how it is. It's so different here than playing back home. Melbourne Park is huge, and everyone is so professional. The girl was really good. A left-hander. Nora Wong. Do you know her?"

Did I know her? I knew her wicked slice serve, that's for sure. "Not really," I said, "but we played her and her sister this morning in the doubles."

"And you won? That's great."

I could see Miri packing up her racket and getting ready to head out. She was checking her phone, her fingers tapping away as she replied to a message. I bet I knew who was texting her.

I peeled myself away from Emily.

"Miri!" I said. "Wait up!"

"I'll catch you later," Miri said, pocketing her phone. "I promised I'd meet someone after the match."

"Who? Dray Yule?" I said, taking a chance. We had to get this out in the open.

Her jaw dropped. Then she scowled. "No, as a matter of fact. Not Dray Yule. If you must know, it's a friend I used to go to school with. Theo's sister, Maria. So if we're through with the third degree, I've got to shower. We're meeting in an hour. At a café on Swanston. Any more questions?"

I shook my head and she stalked off.

chapter eleven

I spent a restless night tossing and turning, my dreams riddled with images of Miri and Dray Yule laughing together as Hamish drowned in the hotel pool. Then Emily Hunt was there, taking my place as Miri's doubles partner, winning the tournament and accepting the trophy that should have been mine. I woke up long before my alarm was set to go off and decided to go for a run. We weren't due on the court until nine thirty. I had plenty of time.

It was a cool, overcast morning, the light still the dull gray of dawn. The streetlights hadn't yet gone out, and the vehicles driving past had their headlights on. There wasn't much traffic, so I darted across Jolimont Road and headed up the much quieter Jolimont Street, jogging easily along the narrow tree-lined road to the footbridge that would take me toward the Yarra River. I'd seen it from my hotel window. A wide, slow-moving waterway that meandered through the high-rises of Melbourne.

It was quiet down by the river, away from the traffic. There was a path that ran alongside the water, and a few people were walking dogs or jogging. A rowing team trained on the river, its boat gliding soundlessly through the water with each stroke of the oars. Melbourne Park and all its complications seemed a long way away.

The air was fresh and crisp. I ran on and on, enjoying the rhythm of my feet hitting the pavement, the pumping of blood in my veins. That was the thing about running. I didn't have to think. My body took over, and my mind switched off. I didn't have to worry about Miri or Dray or Hamish or even the tournament. In fact, all thoughts of them were blown clear out of my head. Until I ran up some steps and found myself in Federation Square, across the street from Flinders Street Station.

I stood and stared at the building, already busy with commuters arriving in the city. Slowly the freshness of the day evaporated. All I could think about was Miri handing Dray that package. I'd thought at first it must be drugs or money or something, but as I stood here now, a horrible suspicion planted itself in my brain. What if it had been more personal? Hadn't Hamish realized his medallion was missing the very next day? The more I thought about it, the more I thought I was right. Miri could easily have slipped it out of Hamish's bag and pocketed it without him knowing. How Miri could have done something like that, knowing what it meant to Hamish, I didn't understand. I stood there until I started to get cold. When it started to rain, I turned and headed back the way I had come.

Miri wasn't in the room when I got back, which was just as well, because I would have confronted her then and there. Given her reaction the day before, who knew what the consequences of that might have been? Remembering Hamish's comments about his racket, I rummaged in the wastepaper basket and found the order form from the restring center. There was Hamish's name, cell-phone number, racket brand and requested string tension, a circle around that number. But the first number had been crossed out and another one written in its place. Someone had altered the docket. I had a feeling I knew who it was. I had to find Miri.

I showered quickly and got into my tennis gear, and then I headed down to the café to get some breakfast.

I was surprised to see Hamish there, sitting alone at a table near the window, finishing off some toast. I glanced at my watch.

"Hey, Hamish," I said. "Did your match get postponed because of the rain?"

"What?" Hamish glanced out the window. The light drizzle that had followed me back to the hotel had stopped. "No, I doubt it. They'll sweep the courts and they'll be dry in plenty of time."

"Then what are you doing here? Don't you play at eight thirty?"

Hamish looked at me like I was nuts. "Yeah. It's only just after seven, Kat. I have plenty of time."

My stomach tightened. "No, it's eight fifteen, Hamish. You should be on the court right now."

Hamish rummaged in his bag and found his phone. "Holy crap," he said. "The clock in my room must be wrong." He grabbed his bag and raced for the door. "Thanks, Kat!" he said as he dragged it open. Then he was gone.

I looked at the remains of his breakfast. If I hadn't come along, he would have finished it off, then wandered over to the tennis center and discovered he'd missed his match. Another part of Dray's plan falling into place, I was sure. But who could have set his clock back? Not Dray, unless he'd bribed a housekeeper to let him in. There was only one person who would have easy access to his room. Miri.

As if thinking of her had somehow brought her to life, I heard her voice outside the café.

"You said he wouldn't get hurt." Her voice was a bit shrill, almost panicky. "A few harmless pranks, that's all."

Sliding into Hamish's seat, I peered out the window in the direction of her voice. Miri and Dray were standing on the sidewalk near the entrance to the hotel. Dray's hand gripped her arm. I wasn't sure what he said, but it must have been something about keeping her voice down, because I couldn't hear any more of the conversation after that. Miri tried to wrench her arm away, but Dray held on tightly. He leaned in close to her and said something more. Even from this angle, I could see how threatening his face was.

I made my way to the door of the café and slowly eased it open. I poked my head out just far enough to get a good view and pulled out my phone. I took a couple of photos, then switched to video. I still couldn't make out what they were saying, but sometimes a picture can speak for itself. After a few seconds, Dray released Miri's arm and she hurried away, heading in the direction of the tennis center.

Dray glanced my way, and I ducked back into the café, my heart pounding. Had he seen me? Quickly I moved up to the counter and looked at the menu board, pretending I'd been standing there all along. But the door to the café stayed closed, and gradually my heart slowed.

I wasn't very hungry anymore, but I ordered a toasted bagel to go. As I left the café, bagel in hand, and started down the street, Dray stepped out of the hotel entrance and blocked my path.

"Kat McDonald," he said. "You've been putting your nose where it doesn't belong."

I tried to look calm, although my heart was in my throat. "I have no idea what you're talking about," I said. I went to move around him, but he sidestepped so I couldn't get past.

"Yes you do. Let's have it." He held his hand out expectantly.

"Have what?" I said, still trying to bluff my way through this.

"Your phone."

"I'm not giving you—"

In the blink of an eye, he had pinned my wrists behind my back with one hand and pulled my face in against his chest. I felt his other hand rummaging through my pockets. I was just about to scream when he released me and stepped back, holding up my cell phone in triumph.

"Give that back!" I said. "You have no right to take that."

"You'll get it back," he said, thumbing through the menu. I tried to snatch the phone away, but he held it high out of my reach. "Ah, here we are." He flicked through the pictures. "You've been busy for quite some time, haven't you?" he said, giving me a glimpse of the photos of him and Colby Barrett. He deleted them with a touch of his finger, then scrolled through again, deleting as he went.

"Now keep your nose out of other people's business." The words *or else* were written on his face.

"Or what? You'll report me for taking photos of the tournament?" I said sarcastically. "Or set my clock back so I miss my match?"

His eyes widened slightly, and I knew I'd hit the mark.

"I can do a whole lot better than that," he said, pointing a finger at me. "You played in the Seattle City Junior Champs last year, right?"

I had. But what was he getting at?

"Yes, I remember you," he went on. "You're the one who got caught smoking weed in the girls' shower room and was banned for the rest of the year."

"I did no such thing!" I said hotly.

He shrugged. "It'll be your word against mine. And you'll be suspended from the tournament while they investigate. It should only take a couple of days."

I glared at him. "I know what you're up to, and it's not going to work. Hamish is good. He'll keep winning. If Colby wants to take the trophy, he'll have to fight it out fair and square in the finals."

"I wouldn't worry about Hamish if I were you," said Dray. "Worry about yourself, because it wouldn't take much to make Hugo Mansfield drop you like a hot potato. And your tennis career will be over before it starts."

He held out my phone to me. "Here. Happy snapping."

I reached for it, but before I could grasp it, he let it slip out of his fingers and drop to the pavement.

"Oh, how clumsy of you," he said and walked off.

My hand was shaking from both fear and anger as I bent to pick it up. The screen was cracked, but the phone still seemed to be working. My other hand still clutched my bagel, now cold and greasy in its bag. I threw it in the garbage and headed for the courts.

chapter twelve

I don't know how I made it through our next match. With no breakfast but one of Hugo's energy bars, I was running on pure anger-fueled adrenaline. How dare Dray threaten me? It was lies, all lies. He probably hadn't even been at the tournament in Seattle. But he was right about the girl in the showers. I'd heard about it too. If he said anything, there was sure to be an investigation. I would be suspended until his accusations were proven false, and that would mean forfeiting a match and losing any chance we had to move into the next round. Hugo would go through the roof, and even though I was innocent, I doubt he'd want to coach me anymore. Not after the stupid performance I'd put on in the qualifier. He had given me a second chance, but if I blew Miri's doubles, I was sure he wouldn't give me a third.

"What's with you today?" asked Miri when we'd finished up, the score a win for us with six games to four. "I've never seen you hit so many winners and make so many unforced errors all in the same game."

"We've got to talk," I said, stuffing my racket into my bag.

"What? But I've got—"

"Now," I said. The look on my face must have told her not to argue.

"Let's go back to the hotel," she said.

"So what's going on with Dray Yule?" I said bluntly when we were seated across from each other on the beds.

"It's nothing," said Miri, unable to meet my gaze. "I went out with him one night, and now he won't leave me alone."

I shook my head in disgust. "Don't lie to me, Miri. He cornered me this morning and threatened to get me kicked out of the tournament. I know you met up with him at Flinders Street Station, and I know he's got some sort of hold on you too. So what's going on?"

Miri's eyes grew wide. She was quiet for a moment. When she spoke, her voice was thick.

"All right," she said, clearing her throat. She looked tense, but her eyes were dry. "I was out with Dray that first night when I broke curfew. We had dinner, and he invited me to this party. There was beer and vodka coolers and—and some pot. I didn't smoke any of it, but I did have a drink."

"Or two or three," I said.

"I know! It was stupid." She covered her face with her hands and shook her head, as if trying to rid herself of the memory.

"I should have just left, but I didn't want to look like a nerd. And once I'd had one, well..." She let her hands drop and took a deep breath.

I waited.

"We got talking," she said. "He seemed so into me. He wanted to know all about me, asked me all these questions. And...I told him."

"And you told him about Hamish too," I said.

Her gaze flicked to me. "Yeah. I don't know exactly what I said. It was the alcohol. I just...talked. I couldn't stop myself." She paused and bit her lip. Like she was deciding whether to tell me the next bit. "And then he sent me the photos."

"Photos?"

She dug in her tennis bag and pulled out her phone.

"You can't tell anyone about these," she said, flicking through the menu.

"I won't."

She glared at me. "No, I mean it. Promise you won't tell."

"All right, I promise," I said. "Let me see."

The first photo showed her sprawled on a couch with two guys, her eyes half closed and drink in hand. It was obvious she was drunk. In the next she was laughing. They were all laughing, like they were on laughing gas...or something else. The last one showed her kissing some dark-haired guy with a shadow of stubble on his chin. I'd never seen him before.

"God, Miri. How could you let this happen?" I said, stunned.

"I didn't mean to," she wailed. "It just— happened. How could I have known he'd take photos?"

I shook my head, hardly able to believe the girl in the photos was Miri. She was usually so in control. So careful with everything. "Why did you go out with him in the first place? I could tell he was a sleazebag the first time I set eyes on him."

She sighed. "I was pissed off at Hamish for chatting up those flight attendants on the plane. I just wanted to give him a taste of his own medicine." She actually looked rather ashamed at this confession.

"But Hamish didn't mean anything by it," I said. "He's nice to everyone. Even me."

I must have blushed a bit, because she gave me a funny look. "You think he's cute, don't you?"

I rolled my eyes, but I could feel the color climbing higher in my cheeks. If anyone ever invents a cure for blushing, I'll be first in line. "Of course I do. He *is* cute. But that doesn't mean I'm going to try to steal him away from you."

She looked down at her fingernails. I could see she'd started to bite them. "You might not, but that doesn't mean someone else won't," she said.

I couldn't believe we were having this conversation. "Hamish wouldn't do that to you," I said. "It's obvious he's crazy about you."

"But why?" she said. "I'm not pretty or smart or funny. The only thing I'm good at is tennis. Why would he want me?"

Was she just fishing for compliments, or did she really believe those things? She looked completely miserable.

"Miri," I said. "Maybe you should take a look in the mirror sometime. Girls would kill to look like you. Your hair is amazing, and you're tall and thin..."

"I wasn't always thin," she muttered. "I used to be fat."

I didn't know if I believed that. I couldn't imagine Miri being overweight, but she obviously thought she had been. I shrugged. "So what if you were? You're not now. And you can be nice. I've seen you with Hamish, and you're always laughing together. He's a good guy. Give him a bit of credit."

Miri bit her lip. I could see she was near tears. "He is a good guy," she said. "That's why I feel like such a shit. Dray is using all that stuff I told him about Hamish to try to get him to lose a match. Did you know there was peanut butter smeared on the lid of that Powerade he put in Hamish's bag? I could smell it. Hamish could have died!"

Well, that was one mystery solved.

"And I took his medallion. And set his clock back an hour." Now that she'd started, the confessions came rolling in.

"But why?" I asked.

"The photos," said Miri. "Dray said if I don't help him, he's going to post them on Facebook. I'll probably get kicked out of the tournament, and Hugo will drop me like a brick, and Hamish..."

I could see her dilemma.

"But we can't just sit around and do nothing. Maybe we should go to Hugo. If you explain everything, I'm sure he'll..."

Miri was shaking her head. "No. No way. We can't go to Hugo. He's got a zero-tolerance policy on alcohol and drugs. He made that clear right from the start."

"Or at least warn Hamish?"

"No! That would be the fastest way to get those photos splashed all over the Internet. We can't tell Hamish."

I thought for a minute, but there didn't seem to be any other solution. "Then we just have to get those photos off Dray. Once they're gone, it'll just be his word against ours. Unless..." I'd done it once. I could probably do it again. "Unless we get some proof of our own."

I told her about the photos I'd had of Dray and Colby Barrett, and the conversation I'd overheard.

Miri looked shocked. "Colby! I knew he was ambitious, but I didn't think he would resort to this."

"It does seem a bit extreme," I said. "I mean, who cares if you're number one or number two in the rankings? It's how you play on the day that counts."

"You don't know Colby's family," said Miri with a shake of her head. "They're old-school tennis from way back. His dad and his grandfather played competitively, and both of Colby's brothers achieved number-one-junior ranking by the time they were sixteen. He's spent his whole life trying to live up to expectations."

"And now he's trying to make sure of it by taking out the competition," I said. "Miri, we can't let that happen. I'll tell you what we'll do..."

chapter thirteen

I went searching for Dray while Miri went to find Hamish and make sure nothing stopped him from getting to his next match. I didn't know how I was going to get Dray's phone, but he would have to meet up with Colby Barrett sometime soon. And when he did, I would be there to video the whole thing.

It took me more than an hour to find him. I searched the courts, the lockers, the food alley. Even sent a kid into the men's bathroom to see if he was in there. Finally, I spotted him coming out of the administration office. The look on his face sent a chill through me. I didn't know what he'd been up to, but he looked awfully pleased with himself.

On the other hand, maybe this was my chance. If he thought he had Hamish wrapped up, perhaps he'd head off to find Colby Barrett and collect his reward. Slipping in behind him, I followed him to the courts. He wasn't in any hurry. He stopped in at the pro shop and chatted to the guy behind the counter for a while, coming out with nothing but a couple of energy bars. Not the kind Hamish liked. The shop was still out of those. Knowing now what was going on, I figured Dray must have bought out the whole week's supply at the beginning of the tournament. He meandered over to court 3, where Colby Barrett was playing singles against a short stubby kid with a freakish ability to get the ball back over the net despite his height disadvantage.

Watching him play, I had to admit that Colby was good. Really good. His serve was textbook perfect and deadly accurate. Maybe not as powerful as Hamish's, but he could place the ball within millimeters of the line. Being tall, he could cover the court in a couple of giant strides, and his basic strokes were as perfect as his serve. I could see why he was a contender for the number-one spot. What I didn't understand was why he would jeopardize his whole tennis career for that ranking when he had the capability to win it on his own merit. Sure, if he made number one, his family would be proud of him. He would have lived up to the family name, shown his dad and brothers that he was as good as them. But if he got it by cheating, he would always know that he didn't really deserve it. And if anyone were to find out he'd cheated...

Dray was on the move again. I shadowed him to the food alley. The smell of fries and donuts reminded me I hadn't had breakfast, so when he got in line at one stall,

I dashed down to Fresh and grabbed a wrap. I didn't want to lose him, but my stomach was growling like a fiend, and I still had another match to play later. Luckily, when I snuck around the corner to have a look, he was still lounging next to the stall, waiting for his burger.

From there he went straight to court 6. Miri and Hugo were sitting in the stands. It was Hamish's singles match. The quarter-finals. If he won this one, he'd move on to the semis tomorrow morning and then the final in the afternoon. I slid into the seat next to Miri.

"Everything all right?" I asked.

"Yeah," she said casually. "No dramas. You?"

I shrugged. "Nothing much happening." I nodded toward the other end of the stands, where Dray was perched in the top row.

Hamish was down 4–3. His opponent was a thin wiry teenager with curly red hair. Before every serve, he pushed it back off his forehead and readjusted his cap. Then he threw the ball up for the toss and launched himself at it like he was charging a dragon. It worked, though. The power he got on his serves was phenomenal. Especially for such a skinny kid.

"Who is this guy?" I asked Miri.

"Owen O'Brien," she said. "It's his first year on the circuit."

I remembered the skinny girl who had partnered with Emily Hunt in the doubles. "Chelsea O'Brien's brother?" She had the same body type as Owen and the same kind of power game.

"How should I know?" said Miri irritably. "He needs to work on his technique."

Poor technique or not, he was playing well. He held serve, and Hamish was down 5-3. I could see Hamish was trying to figure out how to handle this guy. What were his weaknesses? What would give Hamish the edge he needed to win? He couldn't let this kid break his serve again, or he'd be out of the tournament. Which was exactly what Dray Yule and Colby Barrett wanted.

Hamish served, a power shot to the backhand side. The kid blocked it back, setting up Hamish for an easy forehand. Again he powered it onto the backhand. They rallied back and forth on the baseline, time and time again, with Hamish pounding the kid's backhand until finally he got what he wanted. The ball landed short. Hamish ran in and knocked a drop shot over the net.

It was a good strategy. Owen O'Brien loved to slog it out on the baseline. Power was his game, and when Hamish got into a power match with him, they were on a pretty even playing field. Hamish was better than that though. He played Owen's game as long as it suited him, moved him well back behind the baseline, then hit him with something different. A drop shot at the net, a backhand slice, a wide short ball that sent the kid running and more often than not won Hamish the point.

Hamish held his serve easily, and then it was Owen's turn. Hamish would have to change his tactics now. With Owen having the serve advantage, Hamish would have to make sure he didn't set him up for a winning shot with his return.

Hamish's eyes were glued on his opponent as he waited for the serve. Owen flicked his hair back, readjusted his cap. Hamish was on his toes, already moving forward. The ball came at him, hard and wide, but Hamish was there. He returned it crosscourt with a forehand that was almost as fast as the serve had been.

Owen hit it back, fast and deep, trying to draw Hamish into the rally. Instead, Hamish moved around and sent it down the line on the backhand side. A winner.

It didn't take a mind reader to see how desperate Owen was to win this match. It could be the upset of the tournament, one of the top seeds beaten by a newcomer. He adjusted his strings before setting up for the serve, glaring down the court at Hamish like he was trying to psych him out. A quick fix of his hair, then he tossed the ball up for the serve.

An ace. I had to hand it to him. He was good. It takes a lot to ace Hamish Brown.

His next serve was just as fast. Hamish got it back through sheer luck. His return was weak though, straight down the middle of the court, and Owen moved in for the kill. He hit a flat forehand onto the backhand side that barely skimmed the net.

Come on, Hamish, I thought, wanting to scream it out. I wanted him to win so badly, watching the game was almost painful.

Owen O'Brien didn't let up on his power serves. He knew they were his trump card, and I couldn't blame him for using them. They were working beautifully. Luckily, the next one hit the tape and flew out. Second serve. I held my breath. This was Hamish's chance.

The serve landed half a meter inside the service court. It still looked fast to me. I would have had trouble getting it back. Hamish casually pivoted around and hit it with a backhand that had so much topspin, the ball bounced and powered on as if it had hit a turbo booster. The kid clipped it with a one-handed backhand, but it flew out. The score was even again at 30 all.

Hamish won the next point with a drop shot after a long rally, then Owen hit another winning serve straight past him. The score was deuce.

Then it was Hamish's advantage. And deuce again. I was so intent on the game, I almost forgot about Dray. It was only when Hamish had finally won the game with a backhand across the net at an almost impossible angle that I glanced up at the top row. Dray was still there. His face was tense, his hands clenched. I didn't think he'd be going anywhere until this match was finished.

Hamish held his serve in the next game. Owen had a lot of fight in him. He didn't make it easy. And when it was his turn to serve, he ramped up his power serves and aced Hamish three times in the one game. They went into the tiebreak.

There was quite a crowd around the court now. The game had gone over time. The stands were full, and people stood outside the fence, watching the two guys battle it out.

In a tiebreak, the players alternate serving, with each player serving twice before the switch. It didn't leave a lot of room to get ahead. Hamish and Owen fought it out point for point, the scores staying level. I could see they were both tiring. Hamish wasn't moving quite as quickly as he usually did, and Owen's serve was starting to slow. That, if anything, gave Hamish the edge, I thought. The kid's power serve was all that was keeping him in the match.

The score was 9 all, and Owen was serving. He wiped the sweat off his face and adjusted his cap. He looked exhausted. It had been a tough match and had gone way over time. He threw the ball up and brought his racket around. I think he knew when he hit it that it wasn't going in. It slammed into the net.

You could almost see Hamish rubbing his hands together. A second serve was just what he needed. Owen sliced it out wide, but there wasn't much pace on it. Hamish had plenty of time to get there. He did a full backswing, then hit it short over the net. The kid made a halfhearted attempt to get to it, trotting toward the net. He knew there was no way he would make it.

At 10–9, Hamish served an ace and the match was over. There was a huge round of applause as Hamish and Owen shook hands.

"He'll be one to watch over the next year or two," said Hugo.

I glanced over at Dray. He was leaning back in his seat. I thought he'd be devastated that Hamish hadn't lost after all. That was what he was hoping for, wasn't it? But he just sat there. Waiting. For what?

Then I saw. At the court gate, Hamish was talking to an official.

Hugo and Miri went down to see what was going on. I needed to keep an eye on Dray. If he'd had a hand in this, he might give something away.

Miri was back in less than five minutes. Hugo and Hamish had gone off with the official.

"What's going on?" I said. Dray was still in his seat. He looked awfully pleased with himself.

"It's a drug test," said Miri. "Just routine. They do them sometimes. When it gets close to the final." She was trying to sound unconcerned, but I could see she was worried.

"Do they test everybody?" I asked.

"No," she said. "It's a random test. Unless they have reason to suspect somebody. I'm sure it's nothing."

I wasn't so sure. I looked up to where Dray had been sitting, but he was gone.

chapter fourteen

I was worried about Hamish, but there was nothing I could do, and we had a match to play. It was the quarterfinals. I should have been excited. Pumped and raring to go. Instead I felt like I had lead in my sneakers and ice fog in my brain. Miri wasn't on the top of her game either, and between the two of us, we botched up the first couple of games pretty badly.

Our opponents were another pair of sisters, as different from the Wong sisters as you could get. They were both blond, but that's where the similarity ended. The older one was tall, slim and powerful, like Miri. Miri figured she'd be playing her in the semis if they both won their next singles. The younger one was much younger, maybe twelve or thirteen, and still looked like a kid. It was obvious she thought she was pretty good though. She threw a little tantrum whenever she thought we made a bad line call. I thought someone should take her to the optometrist for an eye checkup.

At 4–1, I could see the little kid thought they had it in the bag. And I wasn't so sure I disagreed with her. We'd made stupid mistakes, letting the ball slip through the center line between us, missing easy volleys, lobbing the ball to have it smashed back at us, double-faulting. And double-faulting again. It's those sorts of things that can lose you the match. The sisters weren't winning it. We were losing it. And badly. But the smug look on the kid's face really riled me. So what if she was twelve years old and playing in the 16 and Under?

She just wasn't that good, and without her sister and her own dodgy line calls, she'd have been done long ago.

"That pipsqueak's really starting to piss me off," said Miri as we switched ends. "If she calls one more of my serves out, I'm going to ask for an umpire."

"Tell me about it," I said. "I can't believe she called that last forehand out."

"Tell you what," said Miri with a gleam in her eyes. "We're going to teach that kid a lesson. Pelt her with everything you've got. We'll see how good she really is."

And we did. If she was at the net, we fired the ball straight at her. If she was on the baseline, we made her run. Power forehands, short backhand slices, drop shots. She caught on pretty quickly. She knew what we were doing, and it made her mad. She stamped her foot when she missed a shot, smashed her racket on the court when we aced her. The next time we changed ends, I could hear her complaining to her sister. Loudly. I think everyone in the whole court heard her.

Gradually, we clawed our way back. We weren't playing great tennis, but we didn't stink either. When the score reached 4-5 against us, we thought we might have a chance to win. It was Miri's serve.

She bounced the ball a couple of times, threw it up and served it at about 150 k's to the short kid's backhand. The girl threw her racket out and dived for it.

A perfect serve, I thought.

"Fault!" called the kid.

Miri's jaw dropped, and I think mine did too.

"That was in," said Miri, approaching the net.

"No, it wasn't. It was long." The girl's jaw was pushed out stubbornly.

"It was in," said Miri.

"It wasn't!"

I glanced at the girl's sister. She looked like she wanted to crawl into a hole somewhere.

"Maybe we should replay it?" she said.

"No," said Miri. "I'm requesting an umpire."

It doesn't happen very often, but any player can request an umpire if he or she doubts an opponent's line calls. The hitch is that the umpire comes from the opposing team. Which meant that Miri's umpire was the sisters' dad.

"All right," he said. "Let's finish this off fair and square. I've noticed you two have been playing to Kara an awful lot. Let's keep it clean. No bullying."

Bullying? We were playing to the weaker team member. It was called strategy.

The kid's smug smile as she walked back to the baseline was enough to set anyone off. Miri was smoldering. She smashed a serve at Kara that almost took her head off.

"Fault!" called the umpire, aka Kara's dad. He pointed a finger at Miri. "I'm warning you. One more trick like that and I'll disqualify you."

I didn't know if he could do that or not, and I didn't want to find out. I gave Miri a meaningful look. *Cool it.*

"If she can't handle the hard serves, she shouldn't be playing in the 16 and Under."

Miri was looking at me, but the comment was clearly aimed at the dad. He chose to ignore it.

Miri popped in a soft serve just over the net. The kid ran for it and lobbed it back. Miri could have gone for an overhead smash and probably would have won the point. Instead she hit a soft forehand to the girl, nice and easy. The girl brought her racket back and let fly with a forehand. I tried to volley it, but it flew out across the tramline.

"What are you doing?" I said to Miri.

Miri smiled sweetly. "He said she couldn't handle the power shots. I'm just taking it easy on the poor little thing."

The girl was throwing dagger glares at us now. "Dad!" she whined.

"What?" said Miri. "She can't have it both ways."

"All right," said the umpire. "Enough of the cheek. Just get on with it."

Miri positioned herself on the base-line and served to the older sister, a nice hard serve with just a touch of slice to make it spin. We'd lost any momentum we'd gained in the last few games though. The dad's eyesight was almost as bad as the kid sister's, and a couple of bad shots on our part meant the game was over pretty quickly. We'd lost the match.

I should have been devastated. That was the end of the tournament for me. But as soon as the game was finished, I remembered Hamish and the drug test. It still seemed suspicious to me. Dray Yule had acted too pleased at the end of Hamish's match. I had to find him and figure out what he was up to.

Miri went to find out what was going on with Hamish, and I set off to find Dray. I didn't have time to search the whole grounds again. He could be anywhere. But I had Miri's phone. We'd exchanged phones earlier. I wasn't sure the camera on mine would work after Dray dropped it. I pulled it out now and hit New Message.

Dray. We need to talk. Meet me

Where? It had to be someplace quiet, but somewhere I could easily hide from him.

outside Rod Laver Arena. Miri.

I crossed my fingers and hit Send. That should lure him in. Then all I'd have to do was follow him and hope he did something to incriminate himself.

chapter fifteen

I crouched behind a garbage can just inside the entrance to Rod Laver Arena. There was a wide foyer running the circumference of the building, with concession stands along the outside wall, all locked up with roll-down metal barriers. No one was playing here today, but a tour group had just gone in, and I'd attached myself to the back of the group long enough to come inside without being conspicuous.

Dray showed up about fifteen minutes later. He was in his tennis gear as usual, his sports bag slung over his shoulder. Now that I thought about it, I realized I hadn't seen him on the court all weekend. I wondered if he was even entered in the tournament, or if he was just here to orchestrate Hamish's defeat.

He dropped the bag on the ground, pulled his cell phone out of the side pocket and typed something into the keypad. The next thing I knew, Miri's phone bleeped in my pocket. I swore under my breath—I couldn't believe I hadn't put it on silent mode—then glanced at the screen:

Where the hell are you?

I thought for a second.

Sorry, can't make it. Lost the doubles and Hugo's on the warpath.

Dray called Miri all sorts of unflattering names and grabbed his stuff. He was about to leave when Colby Barrett walked past. Dray hailed him down.

I couldn't hear what they were saying and was about to risk creeping closer when

Dray gestured toward the door to the arena. After a short argument and a quick look around to make sure no one was watching, they came inside the foyer.

I pressed myself further into my hiding spot as they passed within a meter of the garbage can. They walked just far enough inside so as not to be visible from the door.

"So, let's have it," said Dray. "Hamish Brown is out of the tournament. Pay up."

"You don't know that," said Colby. "He could still pass the drug test. In fact, knowing Hamish Brown, I'm pretty sure he will."

"Don't worry. I made sure he won't be getting out on the court tomorrow. I put a joint in his tennis bag for insurance." Dray looked particularly pleased about this.

"You what? That wasn't part of the plan," said Colby. "I just wanted him out of the tournament, not arrested."

Dray glared at Colby. "Don't get all moral on me now. You wanted him out and he's out. Now pay up."

With a look of distaste, Colby dug in his bag and pulled out an envelope. I'd been so absorbed in what was going on that I'd almost forgotten about videoing, but now I grabbed Miri's phone and started filming.

Dray took the envelope and pulled out a wad of money. He counted it slowly, note by note.

"It's all there," Colby said.

"You cut me short once," said Dray. "I'm not stupid enough to let you do it again."

It was then that I noticed Dray's sports bag sitting against the wall. It couldn't have been more than three meters away. It would only take a second to get to it if I could somehow distract them...

I stopped filming and switched to Miri's contact list. There. Colby Barrett. I didn't question why she had his number in her phone. I just hit Text Message and started typing.

I need to talk to Dray. Have you seen him? Miri.

I held my breath and hit Send. Dray was tucking the money into his wallet.

"Miri Tregenza's looking for you," said Colby a second later.

"Yeah?" said Dray. "I wonder what she wants."

So he wasn't admitting he had arranged to meet her here. Interesting. Didn't Colby know about her involvement?

Colby started texting again, and I saw my chance. They were both looking down at his phone, their backs to me.

Heart pounding, I snuck out of my hiding spot, tiptoed to Dray's bag and reached into the side pouch. My hand had just closed on Dray's cell phone when the text came in. Miri's phone vibrated in my pocket.

I should have been expecting it. Of course they were texting Miri. And Miri's phone was in my pocket. But somehow I panicked. Even though the phone was on vibrate, I thought they must be able to hear it, or feel it, or sense it going off, or *something*. I grabbed Dray's phone and took off.

"Hey!" yelled Dray.

I dashed toward the door, but the motion detector was too slow. Dray was after me in a shot. I veered and ran down the corridor. It curved with the circular shape of the building, food stalls on one side, doorways to the arena on the other. Numbers were stenciled on the inside wall to identify entrances to the arena. Bare concrete walls. Nowhere to hide.

With nothing else to do, I ran to the nearest doorway and up a dozen or so steps, finding myself on the second level of the arena. Far below was the court where the Australian Open is played.

I didn't have time to admire the view. I climbed upward, four, five, six rows, until I thought Dray would have reached the stairs, then ducked in behind the seats. My heart was going like a jackhammer. I crawled silently on my hands and knees deeper into the row, crouched low to the floor and waited.

It took less than five seconds for him to figure out where I'd gone. I heard him swear as he entered the arena, imagined him looking around, not seeing me, and starting to hunt. His voice sounded so close, I almost jumped up and started to run again. Basic survival instinct of the hunted. But I resisted the urge and was rewarded with the sound of his footsteps moving off the other way.

Cautiously, I poked my head up and peered over the top of the seats. He was going down the next aisle, searching each row one by one. It wouldn't take long for him to figure out I was on this side of the entrance. Then he would be back.

I crawled farther down the row to the next aisle, holding my breath although I didn't know how that would help. When I reached the end, I poked my head up again. Dray had finished searching the first section of seats and was headed toward the walkway. I ducked out of sight.

Go farther down, I commanded silently, hoping he might somehow obey. *One more section.*

No such luck. He reached the center aisle and paused. I imagined him looking both ways, making a decision. Then he started toward me.

My brain went into overdrive. What could I do? Where could I run? What would he do when he caught me?

That's when I heard the voices. A woman's voice, amplified over a sound system. The softer murmur of other voices oohing and aahing over the arena. It was the tour group, down on the tennis court.

It was exactly what I needed. Witnesses.

I jumped up and raced down the steps. Dray spotted me straight away. With a shout, he thundered after me.

The group seemed miles away. Little action figures moving around on the blue surface of the court. I saw them glance up, point in our direction. It was enough to spur me on.

My feet pounded on the stairs as I sped downward, faster and faster. For once I was glad for all the footwork drills Hugo had insisted we do day after day. No training session went by that we didn't speed step through a ladder or sidestep around hoops or do sprint trials. Now I saw why. My feet were flying. I only hoped Dray had been a bit slack in his training. I felt like he was breathing right down my neck, but I didn't dare look behind me to find out. I didn't dare take my eyes off those concrete steps that seemed to go forever.

At last I caught sight of the walkway at the end of the stairs, and the barrier blocking it from the court. Ten more steps. Five. I glanced up. The court was right below me, maybe two or three meters below the seats. The tour guide was moving in my direction, a concerned and somewhat annoyed look on her face.

I don't know what I was thinking. Or maybe I wasn't thinking at all. I just knew I had to get down to those people. Tell them what was happening. Get them to take me to the administration office, where I could hand over the evidence and keep it out of Dray's hands. I reached the walkway and vaulted straight over the barrier.

The court was farther below me than I'd thought. I'd seen it on TV, during the Australian Open. Seen the winners reaching up to sign autographs after a match, being hoisted up to embrace family members. The barrier between the court and the seats had never looked that high. Now I felt myself dropping down, down and down some more. I landed with a jolt that jarred me right through my spinal cord. My ankle rolled, and pain shot up my leg.

Faces converged around me. The tour guide, with her headset on. Tourists in caps that had *Melbourne* or *Australian Open* blazoned across them. Choruses of "Are you all right?" and "Are you hurt?" and "You poor dear" rang in my ears.

My ankle felt like it was on fire, and it was all I could do not to cry and moan and roll around in pain. Instead, I gritted my teeth and looked straight at the tour guide. "I need to see the tournament director," I panted.

"You're hurt. We need to get you to a hospital," she said. "I'll phone an ambulance and—"

"No!"

I lowered my voice as everyone stopped to stare at me.

"No, thank you. I don't need an ambulance. It's just a sprain. I'll be fine." I struggled to my feet to demonstrate, biting back the scream I wanted to let out as I tried to put weight on my foot. It was probably broken. "I need to see the tournament director," I said, standing on one foot and trying to sound calm. "About the drug testing. For Hamish Brown. He's been set up." I was aware I was spitting things out in telegraphic sentences, but that was all I could seem to manage. "It was Dray Yule," I added and glanced up into the stands.

"Was that the boy who was chasing you?" a man asked. He sounded American.

I nodded, searching the seats for some sign of Dray.

"He took off as soon as you got close."

Of course he did. He wasn't stupid. He wasn't going to hang around and let these people take him in for questioning.

"But I got a great video," the man said proudly. "Man, are you quick."

He pushed Play, and I watched myself racing down the stairs. Dray had been only a few steps behind me right up until I reached the last section of seats and he could see what I was intending to do.

Then he'd stopped, looked around and taken off back up the stairs. I saw myself jump, and then the camera honed in on the ground as the man lowered his hand and ran toward me.

I smiled at the man. "Would you mind coming with me to administration?" I said. "I think your video could seal this case up."

"Gladly," he said.

chapter sixteen

The next day, I crutched my way up the steps to the front row of seats on court 1 and settled in next to Hugo to watch the boys' final.

It had been a long night. After one look at the videos, everyone involved had been hauled in for questioning. Dray, Colby, Miri and, of course, me. The story had been pieced together bit by bit, and once Dray's bag and locker had been searched and his hidden stash of marijuana discovered,

Hamish had been cleared of the charges and reinstated in the tournament.

I'd tried to keep the photos of Miri from surfacing. But when Dray pointed the finger at her for being involved, there was nothing to do but come clean about the whole thing. Dray had blackmailed her into helping him. There was no doubt about that. Of course, the photos put suspicion on Miri for substance abuse, and she was drug tested as well. She passed with flying colors, and because the photos of her drinking were date-stamped prior to the start of the tournament, she was allowed to continue playing.

It was all over for Colby and Dray. I had no idea when, if ever, they would be allowed to compete again. Dray would be facing court for possession of cannabis. As for Colby, his locker and bag were clean when searched, and his drug test was negative for any banned substance. I think we all believed he knew nothing about the drugs. All of us except, perhaps, his father.

I propped my foot up on the railing in front of me. A hairline fracture. I'd be in the cast for six weeks. Hugo had had four long hours in the hospital emergency department with me to express his disappointment. In Miri especially, but in me as well. We should have gone to him in the first place, he'd said. Trust was the basis of all relationships, and if he couldn't trust us, how could he continue to coach us? He needed to know everything that was going on. Everything. No matter how small. It affected our game. How could he help us win if he didn't know what was going on? I didn't know if either of us would survive this. Because let's face it, if Hugo dropped Miri, he wouldn't need me anymore, and I'd be out of a coach.

And that left Hamish. He was mad. Fighting mad. And confused and disappointed and hurt. Miri said they'd had a huge argument after Hugo and I left for the hospital. She'd only just gotten to bed herself when I got back to the hotel. Hamish hadn't said a word to either of us at breakfast that morning, not even when I'd presented him with a half dozen of the energy bars he liked. I'd found them, of all places, in the hospital cafeteria. He looked like hell. His eyes were puffy, and he'd obviously had no sleep. Somehow he'd made it through the semis though, squeaking through on the tiebreak against the number-five seed, a guy from South Australia. So here we were. At the grand final.

Miri edged her way past a couple of spectators and flopped into the seat next to me.

"So what happened with the girls' final?" I asked. Hugo didn't even glance her way, but I got the feeling he was listening.

"Georgia Mason won six to two," she said. "But it wasn't like she was brilliant or anything. I could have beat her. The other girl was crap."

"You didn't beat her," growled Hugo.

Miri had lost to Georgia Mason that morning in the semis. She'd been all over the place. As I said, it was a long night. For everyone.

"You're right, I didn't beat her. But I *could*," said Miri. She leaned forward to look past me at Hugo. "Hugo, you know I could. With everything that's happened, none of us have played like we should have this weekend. But this will never happen again. It was a stupid mistake, and it all spiraled out of control. I won't ever do something stupid like this again. I promise."

Hugo glared at her, and she rushed on. "I'll do whatever you say. Eat what you want me to eat, train whenever you want me to train. You've got to give me another chance."

He continued to look at her until the silence became almost unbearable, then turned his eyes back to the court. "I'll think about it," he said.

It was the best we could hope for. And it wasn't a no, so I was happy.

Hamish put in a valiant effort. He managed to get quite a few aces in the first half, hit some beautiful winners down the line and volleyed spectacularly. But in the end, exhaustion took over and unforced errors started accumulating. His opponent, Ronan Keen, was fresh. He'd won his semis 6–2 and had energy to burn. And as the number-three seed, his skills were almost on par with Hamish's. After the previous night's drama, Hamish just couldn't compete. He lost 6–4.

He looked exhausted rather than disappointed during the trophy presentation. When he came off court, he shrugged.

"It's not all bad news," he said to me when I offered my condolences. "I still made the number-one ranking. Ronan was a few points behind me, so getting second still leaves me on top. If I can hang on to that, I'll be in good stead for the Australian Open Juniors in January."

We gathered our gear from the hotel and hopped into a cab to the airport. Hamish sat in front with the cabbie, probably to avoid sitting next to Miri. He still hadn't said a word to her. We rode in silence until we got on the freeway and the cab picked up speed, weaving in and out of the traffic. Hugo started talking about a tournament in Sydney in December.

"You mean, we're going? Like, with you? You'll still train us?" I said, hardly able to get the words out.

"You'll train in the gym until that cast comes off, and then it's back on the courts. If you can get back up to speed in time, then we'll talk about it," he said.

Miri and I exchanged glances. I felt like high-fiving her but settled for a really cheesy grin.

"One foot out of line, and you're both out," he added.

We arrived at the airport, and I hobbled through the sliding doors. It seemed like a lifetime ago that we'd arrived in Melbourne. The airport was still as busy as ever, the smell of jet fuel and fast food was the same, but I wasn't the nervous little amateur I'd been four days earlier. I knew I'd be back sometime, if not in the next couple of months, then next year. And I knew I'd be able to face whatever the tournament threw at me. Because how could it be any worse than what had happened this time?

Cheating, blackmail, drugs? A mere competition would be nothing. As long as I remembered to eat.

I passed my crutches to the security guard and hopped through the metal detector on one foot. Miri picked up my carry-on for me and we headed for the gate.

"You know, I was thinking," said Miri.

"About what?" I asked.

"About you," she said. "And me."

I waited for her to say something about us making good doubles partners after all, or to thank me for helping her out that weekend, or for being supportive like a friend should.

"If we're going to hang out at tournaments, you really need to get some new tennis outfits," she said. "I don't know when those things you were wearing were fashionable where you come from, but over here we like to update our wardrobe once in a while."

I stopped and stared at her. Was she serious? Then I shook my head. Of course she was. Dead serious. Miri was back.

I did a couple of skip-hops on the crutches to catch up to her, and we hurried on to meet Hamish and Hugo for our flight.

Sonya Spreen Bates is a Canadian writer living in South Australia. She began writing children's fiction in 2001, inspired by her two daughters and their love of the stories she told them. Sonya's stories have been published in Australia, New Zealand and Canada. *Topspin* is her first title in the Orca Sports series.

Titles in the Series

orca sports

orca sports

For more information on all the books
in the Orca Sports series, please visit
www.orcabook.com.